FABLES THAT FOUND ME

TALES OF TORMENT AND HEALING FROM SOUL
(OR SOME OTHER PLACE)

FABLES THAT FOUND ME

TALES OF TORMENT AND HEALING FROM SOUL
(OR SOME OTHER PLACE)

JOE WILLS

First Printing: 2019
ISBN: 978-0-578-46020-8
Joe Wills
6 Governors Lane Suite C
Chico, CA 95926
joewillstherapy@gmail.com

DEDICATION

This book is dedicated to
my wife, lover, best friend, and co-journeyer —
Grace Dorothy Evelyn Wood-Wills

ACKNOWLEDGMENTS

*To Casey Huff, for reading these stories with his eagle eye
and impeccable literary sense*

*To Kate Farrell, who without knowing it inspired me
to take these stories out of the ether*

*To Ammar Changezi, who looking for one thing found another,
these stories, to my great benefit*

To Alan Rellaford, for dressing up these stories in beautiful type

EPIGRAPH

"When you see your matter going black, rejoice —
for that is the beginning of the work."
— Carl Jung

"To truly heal, however, we must say our truth, and not only our regret
and pain but also what harm was caused, what anger, what disgust,
and also what desire for self-punishment or vengeance was evoked in us.
The old healer of the psyche understands human nature with all its foibles
and gives pardon based on the telling of the naked truth."
— Clarissa Pinkola Estés

NOTE TO READERS:

The introduction is a short personal account of what led to my writing these stories. Some of you may prefer to read them without any background and context; if so, skip the introduction.

INTRODUCTION

For many years I kept two fires burning out of sight: wanting to become a great writer, and wanting to fix what I thought was wrong with me. This was a struggle for reasons you can imagine. It is hard enough to succeed in school, build a career, buy a house, marry a terrific woman, raise amazing children – George Bailey's "wonderful life," and "the full catastrophe," according to Zorba the Greek – without all the while keeping two secret fires stoked. I wouldn't say I led a double life (though I will cop to being a Gemini and superhero fan); more it was having two parts to me that felt too frail to fully live out, much less expose to scrutiny. Sometimes people would guess one or other of my hidden callings, smell the smoke as it were. Sometimes this was a great relief, being truly seen for who I was, and invigorating; but other times I felt busted, ashamed, diminished, like the fuel that was feeding the fires had drained out of me. But I would not forsake them, and took solace in the fact that life was not dull or rudderless, and with my two combustible secrets at least I was not water-logged like some blandly content people I knew. (Oh, the judgments!) Yes, even though I kept my fires out of view, they showed up in all kinds of behaviors, decisions and opinions without my knowing it. I could be gratuitously critical of young contemporaries of mine with robust writing careers, not recognizing the envy that drove it. I could be unswervingly helpful and cheerful around people, not aware that their appreciations were sought-after evidence that I had turned into a normal, well-adjusted fellow. Lord knows there are many other examples, but this is an introduction, not an autobiography.

At an early midway point of my life, I entered the dark wood Dante talks about and learned, among many painful and astonishing things, that I had two wrong assumptions about my hidden callings:

I thought my fires were separate.

I thought I had lit them.

During this period, I re-read an unfinished novel I had set aside. I had fashioned it to be wild and exotic, without a shred of my life experience in the plot or characterization. But with the laid-bare vision of a mid-life crisis, I now saw myself on every page. I had a subconscious mind at work! Those weren't just for scary movies, the "Monsters of the Id" from *Forbidden Planet*; I was subject to the same laws of the universe, not some observer whose pen gave him a special exemption. What would be obvious to a reader was not obvious to this writer – my unconscious was projected all over the place in the novel, but until the scales fell from my eyes I could not see it. And the more I read, I could see how I was, without knowing it, trying to work out issues of guilt and anger and self-esteem in those pages. My wanting to be a writer with something to say, and a person who felt OK about himself, had so much overlay I could no longer separate them. I was not full of energy in those dire days, so the fire analogy for my yearnings doesn't seem apt, except for one image, beautifully expressed by Carl Jung, that the purpose of existence is to "kindle a light in the darkness of mere being." Fire seemed beyond me then, but I kept a light going. I clung to the idea that I wanted a challenge-full life, however hard; not mere being, not blandness, but what I ended up calling "really living." Writing and repairing myself could go away and come back as compasses for me, but what I was sure of was this: I wanted the search, the urge, the wish; I wanted wanting. Even when – particularly when – the urge was simply to run my hands through the ashes of my false assumptions and broken certainties. Amid a lot of confusion and doubt, the yearning I felt inside was sacred to me.

Over some time, I had an even more startling revelation about myself. I could welcome my yearning, embrace it, analyze it, even sanctify it, but I could not direct it. I could discover what I wanted, that I wanted; but I couldn't say the wanting was something I controlled. In retrospect, it may seem a natural evolution of the discovery of the mind's unconscious activities to think they are beyond the ego's control; but at the time, and I'm sure some of you know how this feels, it was shattering and humbling. *I* aspired to Salinger-esque prose; *I* had to stop being the fixer and pleaser; *I* had the fire in the belly! Aye yai yai! What saved me and my desperate need to be in charge was being honest about how my yearning expressed itself, how I experienced it. I had to admit it was mysterious. And instead of being scared of the unknown, as I'd always been, I wondered what it would be like to be accepting of it – perhaps it was even another law of the universe. My cosmological view did change, as I saw myself less in the center of things and more just one of the satellites feeling lost but really in orbit, and with plenty of company. I couldn't always see my kindred spirits floating around (Lily Tomlin and Jane Wagner's phrase "space chums" comes to mind), but I knew we were all connected by something. I struggled, still do, with how vague this sounds, yet I ceased feeling so isolated, and more importantly felt my spiritual beliefs coalesce. Luther Standing Bear, the Oglala Lakota chief, author and philosopher, said, "All things were kindred, and were brought together by the same Great Mystery." I take that as an article of faith, nebulous or not.

In coming years, along with spirituality I got more interested in psychology, especially what is called depth psychology, and with that came an interest in dreams. I knew dreams were another mysterious thing that could not be controlled, but I learned that they could possibly be seeded. I read and heard from others that you could set an intention to dream, you could prepare with a journal at your bedside, and in so doing induce more dreaming, or at least more recollection of dreaming. In essence, ask your psyche for dreams, respectfully but importunely, and make some arrangements that show you're serious about it. I tried it, and I remembered dreams – dreams remembered me – more often than before. Paradoxically, while it inched me closer to understanding my unconscious mind, it also helped rehabilitate my opinion of ego: its importance, usefulness, my usefulness. I wondered about setting other intentions, fishing for more connections with psyche, like asking for more conscious awareness for when I had a projection on people I envied or admired, or asking for some deep-seated wisdom during a particularly trying time.

And so we come to the genesis of this book. In the mid-1990s, I had a new position as director of public affairs at California State University, Chico; I was also, along with my wife, a leader-in-training at the Guild for Psychological Studies in San Francisco. My university job was fulfilling and quite demanding; and at the same time, I was totally fascinated by and absorbed in the Guild work, which blended the psychological and spiritual like nothing I'd ever experienced. Unfortunately, soon thereafter I dropped out of the Guild training because I decided to seek another training, to be a psychotherapist, which was just as involving if not more so. My wife and I had been married a decade by then, and worked hard as we still do to nurture a loving and growing relationship; and we had our son living at home going to school and our daughter finishing college and living for a time at home. At such a busy time in my life, and maybe more so because of it, I still had ideas for poems or stories come to me, nudging me for attention. This was a lifelong pattern, ideas coming and me jotting them down; sometimes they were to be found and used later, other times they disappeared, off to join the other missing things in that shadowy band of rebels, the Legion of Single Socks. Anyway, with so much going on, and feeling anxious about it, I asked my psyche for ideas for stories that would be helpful to me, meaning soothing and therapeutic. Necessity liberated me from my usual self-imposed strictures about art; I didn't care if no serious fiction sought out happy endings. If I was to make some time for writing, I wanted some healing stories, as I came to call them, so that I could both enjoy writing and support my anxious self in the process.

It worked. Over what I recall was a fairly short span, the stories in this book came to me – twisting and turning but heading, I kept trusting, toward a place of solace, understanding or redemption. Because I did not have much time to write, it took quite a while for the stories to feel finished. But I am grateful to have had them all these years – old, difficult friends to come back to, time and again. I learned more about writing working on them, they helped me through some bad patches, and I am excited about how their coming into being could be a creative tool to also help clients in my therapy practice. I am grateful.

A bit about the title:

I chose the word "fable" more for its meaning related to extraordinary events, not moral teachings (though I am well-acquainted with Mr. Know-It-All and realize he grabs the pen if I'm not watching). The stories also came to me stripped of details and specifics, like names of things, which I decided not to change, and perhaps this is also redolent of a fable. The word is also, truth be told, alliterative with "found" and I like the music of that. I matched "tales" and "torment" in the title for the same reason. The word torment fits with something all the stories share, but its starting with a "t" sealed the deal. The word tales was chosen because of my love of Chaucer and Hawthorne. You may notice their influence on me as you read the tales that follow.

I may have said enough already about the "found-ness" alluded to in the title – having a story come into my head is so meaningful and visceral and restorative an experience for me that more said might, as Hemingway wrote, "mouth it up too much." I will say that while I feel party to a process that helped bring these stories into being, I have no doubt that they found me or found-out me in a way that is unknowable, and marvelously so. And while I believe that we all share a deep connection, which expresses itself in the common threads through our dreams and myths and stories, I have no illusions that I simply provided a vessel from which these stories emerged. Many magical moments happened with these stories. And I also cleaned up misspellings and took out the extra spaces between the words and sentences. One day years ago I was rhapsodizing how these numinous stories were "flowing through me" and this wise Guild leader, rich with a trickster's spirit, brought me up short by saying, "What a weak ego!" It was just the cold air I needed to be brought back to earth and into my body. I was a writer not a medium. The unconscious and ego both have their parts to play coaxing a story into becoming.

Finally, about the word "Soul":

I can almost remember the first time I used it without my voice trailing off, or without being afraid that someone would ask me what it meant. I have certainly come some miles since then – I put it on my therapy practice business card. I'm still a little halting saying what it means, and that's probably why I put it on the card, to push me and

VI

remind me what it has meant to me, how it has saved my life.

I use soul to describe just what I've been trying to write about in this introduction – the ineffable, exquisite, outrageous particularity that makes each of us who we are, and leads us on the toilsome but enriching journey we take, if we have "ears to hear," as Jesus said. (Clarissa Pinkola Estés calls it soul-hearing.) Soul for me is not ethereal but worldly, impure, complicated and tethered to our collective inheritance, which includes a sack of woes as well as wishes. And the place where the trouble lies is also where the passion lies.

I believe these stories come from soul, but I don't really know, so the title says "Soul (or Some Other Place)." It's a mystery. It also struck me as funny to word it this way… some other place, as in Schenectady? El Segundo? Sometimes you have to laugh. (And I also happen to believe soul loves laughter.) A journey that is hard needs something that is easy, like a chuckle. In truth, I feel we are beckoned to seek what appears to be contrary, but what is, it turns out, exactly what is needed. Heaviness needs lightness. Fire needs water. Hidden needs open. Desire needs action.

And so, my yearning led to this book.

"You cannot by willing it alter the vast world outside of you; you cannot, perhaps, cut the lash from one whip; you cannot, perhaps, strike the handcuffs from one chained hand; you cannot even remake your own soul so that there shall be no tendency to evil in it; the great world rolls on, and you cannot reshape it; but, this one thing you can do — in that one, small, minute, almost infinitesimal spot in the Universe, where your will rules, there, where alone you are as God, strive to make what you hunger for real!"

- Olive Schreiner

THE FUNICULAR

*I*magine *what this will mean to you: You have kept a fortune cookie fortune since childhood. It so perfectly invoked who you were and what you yearned for that it was too precious to part with and too risky to show anyone, lest they scoff at its significance to you. All these years you have kept the slip of paper in a toy treasure chest, seldom seen on a closet shelf but never completely forgotten in its second residence in the back of your mind. At times you have thought about looking at the slip of paper again but you dared not, because to unclasp the chest and expose it to the elements... how would that fortune read now, in the glare of adulthood? Would its magic evaporate into the air before it can be recaptured? And at times you have thought about throwing away the fortune, as a necessary step to accept the limits and lamentations of adult life, but you dared not. Who can say that dreams born of innocence can never come true? Did yielding to the realities of life mean having to say goodbye to the most tender part of yourself? But locked away, neither embraced nor released, years passing by, that fragile piece of enchantment might lose its power anyway, simply by you doing nothing. Banishing thought of your dilemma only brings it back in disguise – contempt for a confident friend, a jiggly leg, a nightmare about the cartoon crocodile who swallows an alarm clock and chases after you. A choice is always there, in the background, in the intersection where you sit with your distractions and irritations. What do you imagine could happen to end the impasse?*

One day I found myself at an airport far from home with time on my hands. The plane was grounded due to equipment problems, and my office naturally wouldn't book another connecting flight because of the added cost, so I had several hours to kill before the new departure time. Because this was a fairly common occurrence, I had a book as well as work with me, and ordinarily I would have bought some food and found a corner of the airport terminal to hole up in until it was time to leave, or if too many thoughts crept into my busyness, I might have veered over to the bar for drinks and cynicism with other passengers. But on this day the experience of being stuck, and how familiar that seemed, made me anxious, and so I left the airport during the delay.

I kept following the exit signs until they led me outside, where I came upon the busy, broad lanes where passengers were being dropped off and picked up. Activity was light, a rare midday Sunday lull. I walked adjacent to the lanes for many minutes, past multiple entrances, under walkways, around construction barriers – it was like being neither inside nor outside, and perhaps for that reason I kept walking, wanting to see more of the sky, and rid myself of feeling trapped, rather than stop and review my strategy for filling up the next few hours. It was not unusual for nervousness and cautiousness to vie for my attention; like a servant with two different masters I answered one bell or the other, without wanting to pick between them or know why they rang in the first place.

While I walked away from the airport, a taxi pulled alongside of me, silently keeping pace though it only seemed so due to the noise of airplanes and automobiles. The driver reached across his cab and rolled down the passenger window. "Where are you going?" he shouted, in a thick, indeterminate accent.

He appeared angry and I thought it was because the queue for taxis was far behind us, while all that lay ahead were exits and on-ramps – nothing for pedestrians. I did not of course know where I was going, except away from the terminal. I tried to quickly weigh my options while he waited, which I knew would not be for long. Go back. Keep walking. Hop in. Not too difficult.

"Don't know where are you headed," he yelled, checking his mirrors. "Come on, I take you where you want to go."

I rarely took cabs, but I couldn't make up my mind so I stepped into the backseat, hastily fabricating a lie. "I thought I'd do some Christmas shopping," I said. The driver was silent for the moment, observing me. I was losing the impulse to leave the airport, and started to ask the driver to just circle back to my terminal. The agitation from being in the terminal was being supplanted by another, missing the flight. But at that moment a call came in on his two-way radio, which he answered in a language unrecognizable to me. Once he was finished, he turned and said, "OK, I take you to an excellent place," and drove off. I asked him to wait, but he smiled and waved his hand at me. "Not very far," he said. I was concerned but instead of insisting he go back I simply gave him the time when I needed to return, and familiarly relied on someone else's authority over my own. He nodded to me like he understood when I said the time, which I took to be reassuring. Resigned to the circumstances, I settled into my seat.

I absently peered between the front seats -- the passenger side was draped with a flowered sheet acting as a seat cover. The glove box was open and figurines – little statues, toys, crude sculptures – were propped up inside, as if arranged in a scene. The dashboard had framed snapshots of people, places and objects on it that were somehow affixed to stay put like the statues. I took out the pocket-sized spiral notebook I carried with me to make reference to the cab's interior; it was the kind of thing that might make an interesting story. I opened to a page with a list of items to bring on the trip – dop kit, business cards, dress shoes and such – each of which had been crossed off that

3

morning. The facing page had a list of similar items from a trip the prior month. Thinking about the lists, and how little they and the job that generated them meant to me, I lost interest in writing anything about the cab and put the notebook away.

Outside the taxi window were road crews, strip malls, busy intersections. We got on a freeway surprisingly devoid of traffic. Staring out the window, and possibly put at ease because of the progress we were making, I drifted off. The next thing I recall the taxi was stopped and the driver was turned around in his seat. He told me where I could walk nearby and get to a market with things from all around the world; and how close from there I could take either a taxi or bus to go back to the airport. They were pretty elaborate directions, but despite his limited English I mostly understood what he was suggesting I do. The odd element was a train he said I should take from the hill we were on down to the market. He held his hands apart several inches as he said the word "train," wanting to indicate that it, or the distance it traveled, was short. Then he put one hand above the other and simultaneously angled one hand in an upward motion and the other downward. He repeated the action while struggling with a word that sounded like "funeral." I was confused, not to mention concerned, about the juxtaposition of "train" and "funeral." I think he saw this so he added, "One must go up while the other down – you will see." I didn't believe any more explanation would be helpful, and the clock was ticking to make my flight, so I paid him and got out.

It was an imposing, intriguing area – tall buildings of all architectural styles, views in all directions – but I was intent on following the course the cab driver had set for me, if for no other reason that it would put me in a good place to get transportation back to the airport. Where he had dropped me was more or less a dead end;

ahead was a concourse designed with public art, plants, and a fountain outside of several multi-story buildings. I skirted all of this until I came to a brightly colored little building with pillars and turrets at the edge of the hill. It looked like something you would see at an amusement park, and in fact there were people inside lined up. Getting closer I could see there were steep train tracks leading down to a street below and two small rail cars, each slowly heading in opposite directions. This clarified what the cab driver had been trying to tell me, and I got further explanation when I heard a man leaving the station say it was called a funicular railway, where cables attach to two rail cars that travel in opposite directions, counterbalancing each other. I was amused the driver had even made an attempt at saying the word funicular.

One more group rode down, then it was my turn. From a platform you stepped into a rail car that was built parallel to the hill, to be only used on an incline. The little wooden benches inside were level with the platform so you could go down the hill without being pitched forward, and every bench had a metal pole by it to hang onto; otherwise, the car fit what you would imagine a quaint little trolley would look like. I was focused on where we were headed, and what time it was, so when the door closed I was surprised to see only five other people had boarded: a middle-aged man wearing a black leather jacket, smoking a cigarette; a younger woman in a lab coat, holding a flower in her hand; an old couple, both with far-off looks, clutching each other; and a spellbound boy staring out the trolley window. We descended the hill and exited in silence. The ride took just a few minutes – the track was only about the length of a football field. As the cab driver had said, there was a popular destination nearby, a big, eclectic market across the street, primarily produce stands and eateries, a real crossroads for people of various nationalities and ethnicities. After one circuit around the market I walked down the street as directed and easily caught another cab to take me back to the airport.

I had to hurry to the gate to make my flight. It was crowded, and my seat assignment was in the rear where it was loudest. To be expected, the engine noise at take-off was deafening, and it seemed to lessen only slightly as the flight continued. Night fell, and the lights were dimmed after meal service. I normally didn't sleep on airplanes, but it may have been that the thrum of the engines, as loud as it was, had a soporific effect on me. And it was a long flight.

I was deep asleep when I was awakened by turbulence – not the typical bumps and dips but major jolts that quickly led the captain to ask passengers to return to their seats. It was black outside the window except for bright flashes of lightning. The jet engines screamed as the plane banked to one side, presumably to get away from the storm. We stabilized, then lost altitude instantly creating a roller coaster-like weightlessness that brought muffled cries from passengers and sent drinks bouncing off tray tables. Two flight attendants who were near me collecting cups at the back of the plane immediately sat down in the middle of the aisle. They looked concerned, which led me to be concerned as well. Lightning streaked brilliantly just off the airplane wing. It was bright enough and long enough to see sheets of rain illuminated. I thought it was too cold to rain at high altitudes, which made me wonder how much we had fallen. Whether we were still dropping or leveling off it was impossible to say, with the din of the engines and the storm buffeting the plane. After one powerful bolt of lightning the cabin lights flickered. A woman screamed nearby, and I reflexively made a loud, brief groan in response, a sound I didn't recognize in myself. I did not feel dread, which was familiar, but something even more visceral, and new. We could crash, I heard myself saying, or thinking. Panic took hold – my heart pounded, I gripped the armrests, my palms slickened with sweat, I could not concentrate. Each second was suddenly stretched beyond its borders. I felt alone and vulnerable and inconsequential. I knew no one on the plane, had said no goodbyes, was reminded by a sardonic inner voice that I had not accomplished anything in my life, or attained what truly was my heart's desire – I could not force myself to recall anything positive or reassuring. Images ran through my mind without sticking, except for one: the five people on the funicular. What a cruel bit of humor, a joke on the way to the gallows: my mind fixing on a group of random strangers, and not some signal idea or person that was vital to me. It seemed the height of absurdity, a testament to what was ultimately, apparently, a meaningless existence. I pictured the five of them, going about their lives that evening, oblivious to having crossed paths hours earlier with someone killed in a plane crash. For some reason I could see them clearly in my mind, doing mundane things and coping as best they could, with me eavesdropping unbeknownst, using some special dispensation that people in life-ending moments have. And I was pleased they wouldn't know about me, wouldn't fret over me, wouldn't reflect on the tragedy, and not because it confirmed the meaninglessness and randomness of life, but because I wanted them to be free – free of the crash, free of me, free of any bad juju that might have been tagging along with me. I wanted these five people to make something of their time on the planet, to reach their hearts' desires – it was a cockeyed, maudlin wish, as I saw it then, but it made me happy, and calmed me down, amidst the chaos of the plane. I took a deep, satisfying breath. I was alive, and calmer for it. And then the plane's engines throttled down, the buffeting lightened, the flight attendants got up, and the captain came over the intercom to tell us, as only an airplane pilot can, that that little bit of trouble we had back there was over and everything was set for landing. I laughed but it was not really sarcasm – more relief, appreciation, and joy. Outside the window below, points of light started appearing, the galaxy of streets and houses and businesses where we were headed. I took a furtive glance at the passengers seated around me, who had receded from view during my desperation and now, like the signs of life on the ground, were present again. I straightened my jacket, wiped my face with a napkin and generally began composing myself for leaving the plane and re-entering the unexceptional world.

In the days after the flight I was light-hearted and optimistic, and enjoyed recounting to people my harrowing adventure once I'd returned safely home, particularly comforted by the fact that I had no more out-of-town business planned in the near future. Resuming my daily routine, the positive emotional bounce from the averted disaster gradually faded. Normalcy, meaning the way I had lived before, returned. But I was not untouched by the flight. While I had no more of the panic that struck during the scariest moments, I noticed just thinking about it brought an unpleasant echo of the experience, a skipped heartbeat, a flushing sensation in my forehead and scalp – it felt like a door had been opened that would not completely shut anymore. It was frightening to me that I might only have this new aspect of anxiety as a result of what I'd gone through on the plane, that the totality of what happened could have a net negative impact on me, and not alter the course my life had taken in a providential way.

It was during a monthly staff meeting I attended – large group assembled, long agenda to plow through – when the first tale came. I still occasionally thought about the five strangers on the funicular, mused about their whereabouts, remembered wisps of dreams about them, but that day, out of the blue, I had a story about one of them in my mind. I'm sure my co-workers sitting around me must have wondered what prompted all the note-taking, because I started filling up a sheet on my legal pad. It was not an idea for a story, or the start of a story, but something astoundingly whole and complete, like Athena emerging ready for battle from Zeus' head, though that was an illusion since the words were not yet written, the clay not yet applied to the armature. And I don't mean that the story was complete in terms of detail, such as names and places and dates; more in the sense of what would or could befall this person I had glimpsed on the trolley. I tried to write as fast as possible, and I'm sure it looked odd in the middle of an otherwise unremarkable office meeting, but I didn't care. When the meeting broke up, I avoided any interactions and decamped to my office, and kept going. At some point I had to stop for work reasons, put an ellipsis on the end of the most recent line, and wait for my next opportunity, hoping I would not lose the thread of the story. All of my feelings that day, the urgency to write, the disregard of my job, even the angst about getting the story down on paper, were welcome. At home I continued into the night until the tale to its conclusion was written.

A day or two after that, another story, about another of the funicular riders, came to me. I was just waking up and grabbed a pen and paper, whatever was handy, and began writing in bed. I called in to say I was not feeling well and would not be coming into work. In fact I felt beside myself with excitement, holed up with another story to tell in my head. Hours passed as I wrote. Like the other tale it was by turns strange and satisfying, recognizable and unpredictable, but never out of reach. At midday I happened to look up at my half-opened bedroom door, and sunlight was hitting it in such a way that the vague contours of a person – head, torso, arms – could be construed. The quality of the light, the grain of the wood, the angle of the door could all explain the shape I saw; but it did not explain that the image unmistakably fit the person whose story I was writing. On another day I might have dismissed the possibility, blamed it on drinking or poor vision, laughed about it like someone's home-grown tomato that took the shape of an angel. But on this particular day I accepted what I was seeing, and was not spooked by it, just as I was not by the sudden manifestation of stories in my head. They had touched a redoubt of faith long hidden from view, and scarcely acknowledged: that I secretly hoped for some sign of wonder and mystery in the world. The preponderance of years may have deadened the wish, but with pen in hand, and the image on the door, the passage of time and my rote cynicism seemed no barrier at all. Here it is, what I've been waiting for, I thought. I felt an exquisite tingling around my eyes and thickening in my throat, abruptly full of emotion but pleasurably so.

It took another few weeks for tales about the remaining funicular riders to show themselves. Perhaps because I was somewhat anticipating them and had an expectation about their shape and scope, or perhaps because I was not so awe-struck when the moment came, I felt more involved in the direction of the stories as I wrote them down. But the experience of being connected to something wondrous and outside of myself was still there. Even when I was not writing, that sense lingered, of not being completely in charge, not needing to be, and happily so. When I took a vacation from work to look at what I had written, I felt immersed in the connection, this lovely mystery I now had in my life, but I didn't vacate who I was before the stories began. I didn't quit my job, leave town or stop shaving. My caution and worry hadn't taken a holiday, but now struck me, curiously and pleasantly, as evidence of how serious I was about what I really wanted, rather than how removed. They were onerous for a reason, calling attention to the choices I made, in service to my deeper wishes. Viewed in this light, they remained but in a defanged state.

When I was finished writing the tales down I spread them out in the middle of my living room floor. The bulk of the pages and my sense of accomplishment were thrilling, so long I had wanted, but struggled to find, the agency to write. Most of the paper came from pads and notebooks of similar sizes and colors but each sheet had a particularity when I looked at it; something more than just the time, place and manner of my writing. Maybe it was pride, or that an air of enchantment still clung to me. I sat with my eyes on the paper, almost expecting it to collate itself or do some other trick from an apprentice magician. In time, though, I realized I was not finished, that a next step was required.

Many thoughts about what to do crossed my mind before one took hold. After a house and yard forage and a trip to the hardware store I had two pulleys, four spools, ten feet of rope, an old piece of plywood and two six-pack beer cartons. I screwed the pulleys into the plywood across from each other about four feet apart, and the spools on either end and below the pulleys, so there was a triangle at both ends. I passed the rope through the two pulleys and around the spools, so that when the ends met there was a hexagon shape, with two terminals and two parallel tracks of rope separated by about 20 inches. I then fed the line through the cartons, one on each side of the parallel tracks so they were opposite each other, before tying the rope off. Several test knots and a liberal use of duct tape were needed to get the rope taut and the cardboard cartons steady, respectively. I propped the plywood up on a bookcase and slid the rope back and forth, moving one carton up and the other down. With some imagination you could see it had the action of a funicular. The weight of the descending car lifting the ascending one. A cable of many strands passing through it all.

I rolled up the pages of the stories and fit them into the squares of the six-pack carton that was on the downward line, imagining the tubes of coiled paper as stand-ins for the passengers. I thought about drawing some features on the rolls of paper, but instead names – actually descriptors – came to me: For the woman in the lab coat, who wanted to create something no one had ever seen, I wrote The Alchemist; for the boy who became a man with a desperate object of desire, I wrote The Coveter; for the old couple who kept to themselves after experiencing life as outcasts, I wrote, on their two rolls, The Shunned; and for the man in the black leather jacket who left polite society behind, I wrote The Bear. It was bizarre how I felt I knew them, these people I did not know at all, and would likely never see again. And yet it was equally bizarre to claim the tales as purely my own invention, the five passengers my fantasy brethren and nothing more, as if the stories had not felt whole when they came to me, and I was not beguiled by the synchronicity of events that had wonderfully taken hold of me. If I was the one who had chosen the words for the tales, it felt instead that they had chosen me. If I was familiar with these creations, I was wholly unfamiliar with their true creator, the source of the fertile and mysterious place I was in, about which I knew nothing except what could be presupposed by the writing in front of me.

I looked at the coiled pages packed into the carton, regarding them intently, wondering and waiting. I began to envision the passengers as a group, with more than a short trolley ride's opportunity to be together. What if they had the benefit of time, with all they had and would experience: What would they say to one another? What would they say to me? I stared at the one empty space in the six-pack carton, where I would go. I was the sixth person on the funicular, but I had no written story of my own. Something must go there. What? I felt a tightening along my scalp, and, breathing deeper, hoped anxiousness might direct me rather than distract me in the moment. On my feet, I wandered around like a dowsing rod, trying not to think but merely notice – a sign, a clue, a whiff of the numinous. In the kitchen, there was the white plastic pasta grabber I used as a back scratcher; in the bathroom, the bronze hand mirror with a green patina found in an alley; in the bedroom, a battery-powered faux candle that flickered in poor approximation of the real thing. All might fit in the empty space of the beer carton, and all seemed more ridiculous than numinous as stand-ins for me. I smiled, trying to be gentle with myself, and in so doing noticed my roaming had evoked a memory of playing hide and seek as a child, which led me to enter my bedroom closet, where I crouched down so I could squeeze in and pull the door closed. The darkness was inviting but crouching made me feel uncomfortable and small, and with my body pushing clothes off of hangers, silly and self-conscious as well. As I stood up and raised my hands to try to avoid more clothes hangers, I knocked something off the closet shelf above. I reached for the door knob to dispense with this foolishness, and then in my mind's eye I had an image of what I kept on that shelf, the thing I was looking for without knowing it, what I was seeking all along. I reached up in the dark, knocking more stuff off the shelf in the process, before I found it. Stepping gingerly, cradling it, I went back to the living room and the funicular. My hands shook as I opened the clasp. The little slip of paper sat in the treasure chest, just where I had put it so many years ago, weathered but intact. I picked it up, it did not crumble; I turned it over to read, it did not fade. How fortunate,

I thought, chuckling at my little pun; I was amazed, or maybe not, how it brought back the lump in my throat and the tingling around my eyes. I carefully balanced the slip of paper face up on two sides of cardboard where the open sixth square of the carton was. It was dwarfed by the rolls of story pages beside it, but it was so much bigger than the seven words written on it, and so much more telling for how long I'd had it, and how I'd been stymied by it, until now. And it was only the beginning. *Imagine what this will mean to you:* It was the first line of my tale.

THE ALCHEMIST

One day, a professor wondered: What if I created flowers? It was not a strange concept, but it struck her like a thunderbolt. For quite a number of years she had taught science at an average, medium-sized university. She was tired of the demands of academia, the need to publish for promotion, sit on unproductive committees, teach packed classrooms of uninspired students, and in the meantime try to have a rewarding life outside of work. She was also a single mother, on top of everything else – she had long ago given up trying to provide enough attention for her moody daughter, who was off at college surely regaling her friends with tales of her unhappy childhood. No, for someone with her education and training she was underpaid and underappreciated. A modicum of respect came with university teaching, but it was increasingly perfunctory. Those students of hers who bothered to get to class and stay awake said the word "Professor" before her name, if they knew her name, so mush-mouthed and blank-faced that there was no possible meaning in it for them. Her title, like her salary, was not nothing but still was ultimately unsatisfying. And there was not another university she could go to, because they had their own cadre of professors, they did not need or want her, nor were conditions at those schools any different. For all the supposed stature of a faculty appointment, she was effectively trapped. Over the course of her discontent she had not seen any means of escape, until this very moment.

She believed she had all the tools to create flowers. She had knowledge of genetic engineering, grafting and hybridizing; she knew how big research laboratories operated; she was conversant with flower and seed companies: Put it together, and perhaps it spelled success. Success beyond anything academia could hope to provide.

In her small amount of free time, she drafted business plans, applied for venture capital, and contacted entrepreneurial centers. It was work, but rewarding all the same; in this arena, the stakes were unquestionably higher. She was not submitting a research paper to a journal that did not pay its authors, she was sending in proposals that could possibly reap her large sums of money. And everyone at the other end of her business inquiries knew that, and accepted that – they were looking for the same thing she was. It was as if she had found the right crowd, finally, to associate with. So the extra work did not bother her.

As plans progressed, it became clearer and clearer that what she lacked was a niche, something unique to her business. Gradations of newer or better flowers would not make it. The giant agriculture firms would create the disease-resistant species and the best producing seed populations; she could not compete with their mass-marketed, capital-intensive efforts. She needed a big idea, some compelling thing. It would take inspiration, which made her wince. Inspiration had never been her strong suit. She was a plodder, a measurer, an A-to-B kind of scientist, which was how it should be: Knowledge built brick by brick. But she was also not a patient person, and she knew something else was now required. She thought about the story of Archimedes in his bathtub screaming Eureka! when he realized what the displacement of water meant. Did those moments really happen? Maybe to other people.

She went about her university activities wondering if the inspiration would strike. Each daily annoyance – signing student add/drop forms, looking for a parking space on campus – felt like an impediment. One day walking through the school's rose garden she dropped the papers she was carrying. While hastily retrieving them, she cut her finger on a thorn. Her anger welled up and she batted a rose bush with her shoulder bag. What a waste, to have beautiful flowers cursed with thorns. As she stood up, it came to her: She should create the perfect thornless rose. Rid the world of the irritation that ruins the rose's charms. Why should you have to open a vein to reach out and grasp a handful of beautiful roses? Sure, there were roses without thorns – there were more roses than there were words to name them – but not like these, she thought, looking around the lush rose garden. No one had created a rose without thorns that would replace all roses with thorns. Once she had gone public with the thornless rose, there would be other flowers to create; but this one would be her signature, this one would tell the public who she was, and what she was capable of doing.

She looked around, seeing if anyone had been watching her, as if her idea was somehow self-evident and available for the taking. In fact, she was alone. She relaxed, and said, barely audibly, Perfect. The part of the quadrangle where the rose garden lay was a particularly scenic section of campus. She chuckled, remembering a black comment a colleague had once made: A university is a great place without students around. It struck her that the thornless rose was the same – a state of being people dared not wish for: all the advantages, without the drawbacks. She could give that to people, she thought, and with that idea stirring her, she swept up the rest of her papers and briskly walked on to her office.

That night, she decided to congratulate herself on her inspiration with a little party. She went back to the rose garden and cut a bouquet of roses – only the university groundskeepers were supposed to do that, but she doubted anyone would question a biology professor.

She stopped at the gourmet shop on her way home to buy an expensive bottle of wine and a few chocolate truffles. After bringing in a vase from her garage, she really looked at the roses she had cut. She had never had roses around her house; that reminded her of her grandmother's house, with pink bathrooms, frilly bedspreads and heavy velvety curtains. The rose had always been an old lady's flower to her – that was why she had always hated roses: They were so blatantly feminine, and she didn't like that. She wore pants instead of skirts, avoided make-up and kept her hair at a short, serviceable length.

She sipped her wine in the living room while listening to some soft jazz and staring at the roses she'd gathered in a glass vase. Finally she lifted a single stem out and brought it under her nose. She inhaled deeply. It was truly intoxicating. She held the rose to her nostrils, then trailed it past her mouth and chin. One petal fell to the floor in a pirouette. She examined the bloom closely and slowly pulled the rest of it apart, letting the other petals fall into her lap. While she had thought it was scientific impulse, the act of taking the rose apart petal by petal became increasingly sensual. It reminded her of a time many years earlier when a man she barely knew had taken her home with him and undressed her. She generally hated not being in control, but what he did had made her flush with arousal, and the memory of it did likewise. She had closed her eyes while he fluttered over her skin like a butterfly. He was already naked to the waist and she had glimpsed his thickly muscled upper body – the erotic tension of those muscles moving lightly over her skin was excruciating. When he brushed her breast with his smooth cheek she actually gasped.

She thought about that as she pulled another rose apart – all its secrets revealed. But the difference was, it could not be put back together. Fragile, like a flower… This was not a bad thing, she thought.

A fabricated rose was not valuable. She reflected on the silk flower arrangements she saw in cheap restaurants – they were like wallpaper. Real roses lose petals when the time has come, the value inherent in millions of years of evolution.

The rose smell hung on her as she walked around her house with another glass of wine. All the matronliness of it faded, replaced by a sense of power. Femininity was a form of power, she thought. She tried to recall an odd short story she'd had to read in high school, about a girl who exuded a flowery scent that seduced men and slowly poisoned them. She smiled at that image. Women who had strong perfume on their bodies seem to say, Don't play around with me. The rose was like that: I am beautiful… but be careful, I can hurt you. For a moment she wondered if she was doing the rose wrong by defanging it. Then she concluded she was merely transferring the power to the woman who owned the flower. The flower's strength was now her own. She imagined having the thornless rose in her lapel, and men wanting to fondle it. Handle with care, she thought, giggling at the prospect.

In the weeks to come, the memory of her celebratory evening drifted away as the hard work began. She had her garage converted into a lab work space with bright lights, all-weather carpeting and climate-controlled air conditioning. She added a small greenhouse that was accessible from a side door to the new lab. She acquired the necessary plant stocks and seeds, tools and equipment. Soon the smell of the roses she kept in vases blended in with the odor of chemicals and machines. In one corner of the lab space hung a wipe board, which in her teaching life would have held class assignments and other instructions to students; here it tracked the goals and progress of her own soon-to-be-successful business.

In the beginning she worked in fits and starts when her teaching and other professorial duties allowed. As time went on, however, she took every opportunity to work in her converted garage. She was supposed to accompany a friend shopping one Saturday, but she lied about coming down with a cold and stayed home to plant some fresh seeds. Sundays she liked to go downtown and meet her friend for breakfast, but gradually she gave that habit up, and chose to hunker down in her lab instead. She liked that she'd kept her new venture a secret from friends and colleagues; she felt like she was in a bubble, able to think big and act creatively free of their doubts and jealousies.

On a rainy afternoon, returning home from a professional conference, months after deciding to create flowers, she saw in the greenhouse the first fruits of her labors. One plant she had grown had a spectacular bloom and a smooth, unblemished stem. She could not keep quiet – after so many voiceless hours hunched over a work bench or potting box she screamed in delight at her triumph. Her thornless rose! She stripped off her coat and hat and flung them over her head. Her hands went around the tallest stem, giddily rubbing its waxy surface with no chance of being pricked. She exulted in how many people would want this flower, how it could bring her wealth and freedom from her dead-end faculty job. Rosa emancipatia! The rose petals were flaming red, as soft as down. A whiff was like being connected to an electrical outlet.

Practically running into the lab, she grabbed a pair of clippers, and cut the tallest stem from the rest of the plant. She held it under her arm while returning to the lab and rummaging in a tool drawer until she found what she was looking for – a ball of string. She cut a long length and tied it at one end just under the glorious bloom. Standing on a stool she looped the other end around a beam and knotted it so the stem hung from the ceiling. She moved the stool and looked up: Her trophy rose swung lazily on its axis, surveying the lab and its contents.

She left for the kitchen beside herself with glee. She uncorked a bottle of champagne she'd been keeping in the refrigerator and poured a glass while contemplating calling her friend with the exciting news. Several times she picked up the phone but put it back down, as there was much more explaining to do than she felt capable of, bouncing around the house in a state of exhilaration. She could talk to her friend and tell her what was going on another time, not when she could scarcely sit still. Too energized to eat, too diverted to bother with a coat, she drove in the rain to her health club and worked on the weight machines. She hardly felt an ache in her muscles as she went from station to station. It was only after a long, hot shower that she began to settle down. She treated herself to dinner at an upscale restaurant, then went to a movie. But she could not concentrate on it, thinking instead about the production and marketing plans she had written for her business that could now be put into motion. She went home and sat up in bed re-reading them until sometime after midnight she finally turned the light off with the papers strewn about her. She lay under the sheets wide awake, fantasizing about the moment when she would walk into the dean's office and announce her departure from the university. How delicious that would be! His muted expression of surprise trying to mask signs of newfound respect, and then grudging envy... she was awake many hours before finally falling asleep.

Unfortunately she had to teach a nine o'clock class the next morning but couldn't resist peeking at her flowers when she woke up. Traces of a dream, where she was floating on a cushion over a lovely meadow, sifted through her consciousness. As much as the dream pleased her, the thought

21

of her new rose beckoned that much more. She bounded down the stairs, clicked on the heater, then headed toward her creation in the greenhouse.

She saw the unsettling sight through the open lab door immediately, transfixed in her bathrobe with a nighttime headlamp illuminating the scene: The petals of the new thornless rose she'd put on display had turned black and fallen on the floor. The rose stem, with only a few withered sepal leaves left on it, still hung on the string attached to the ceiling. Under it were the dark, desiccated pieces of what had been a scarlet halo of beauty.

Perplexed, she leaned over the fallen petals and touched one. It barely moved. She tried to pick it up, disturbing it as little as possible. It was stuck in the drab carpeting she had put in for the lab to cover the garage's concrete floor. She gently tugged at the petal, hoping to keep it intact so she could better examine it, but it stayed rooted to the spot. Another petal next to it behaved the same. She had never seen anything like this. It was one thing to have roses turn a little black from frost or sun or bugs or diseases, but this was a healthy bloom hours earlier. Plus nothing she knew of would explain why they were stuck in the carpeting. What kind of flower had she created? What else did she not know about this new business? Her throat was tight, making it hard to swallow, and her stomach felt queasy.

She quickly washed her hands in a basin in the lab and went into the house. She dressed in a rush, and left without her customary cup of coffee. While she had forgotten it, she was too unsettled to drink it, anyway. She realized as the car warmed up in the driveway that she did not have her books for the morning class. They were lying in the front hallway but she did not go back in the house to retrieve them. She felt slightly better when she reached her campus office, but she was still flustered – she approached her office feeling exposed, as if her bizarre experience that morning was written across her face, and she would be forced to say something about it, and then recount her secret work. She called her department chair and said she did not feel well, and asked if she could cover the class for her. She stumbled telling her where they were in the syllabus and what assignments were due; the information seemed to be in a far corner of her mind. After hanging up the phone she sat watching her hands fidget on top of a pile of student papers. Eventually she wrote an e-mail to the students in her two o'clock class, telling them it was cancelled and rescheduling some due dates for work until the following week. At that point she had a cup of tea in the department office, and rather than answer questions from the staff and her colleagues about how she was, she went back home.

The overcast sky lightened on the drive back, and she reminded herself of what she had learned about science in graduate school, and what she often told her students: Re-work the process. Learn from your mistakes. One step forward, two steps back. Where in her research and development had she gone wrong? she thought. This line of thinking comforted her a bit, and bolstered her confidence. She never thought it would be easy to create flowers and change her life. But as she returned to her house, she was still not eager to resume work. She went upstairs to her bedroom, where her bed was cluttered with her business papers. She carefully straightened them up and placed them in their proper folders. She read over some of her outlines and timetables for success. She was suddenly very tired and dozed off curled up on her bed.

When she awoke later that day, she went downstairs to a dark house. She lingered outside the door to the lab. The image of what lay beyond the door swept away the after-effects of her nap. She walked around turning on lights, adjusting the thermostat, putting on a pot of water for coffee, finding little things to do. At no time did the fallen rose petals leave her mind completely. She sat at her kitchen table and began to sort through a stack of envelopes that had accumulated, tossing the junk mail into the garbage, waiting for the water to boil. When it did, she got up to take the whistling kettle off the heat, and as she slid the kettle to another stove-top burner, she caught the edge of the kettle on the heating coil. Hot water spurted out of the spout and onto her wrist. She stamped her foot and yelled out in disgust. She held her wrist under cold water, but it did nothing for the anger she felt. She pounded the cabinet above the stove with her palm. She turned around and grabbed a grocery store flier addressed to "Occupant" and reduced it to shreds before throwing it into the garbage container. A few scraps ended up scattered on the floor, and the way they were arrayed reminded her again about the rose petals in the lab.

Moving rapidly, she went to her hallway closet and pulled out the vacuum cleaner. She dragged it into the lab, plugged it into a wall outlet, and turned on all the lights. The fallen petals were gnarled and impenetrably black in the stark lighting. She turned on the vacuum and rolled over the petals, again and again. Bits of them disappeared, but many remained. She turned off the vacuum and went down on her hands and knees to pick at what was still stuck in the carpeting. Without cutting into the pile of the carpet, it was useless to try to get it all. She stood up and vacuumed again, then surveyed the area – it was better, but remnants of the rose were still imbedded in the carpet. A diminished presence, but a presence nonetheless. She put the vacuum away and sat at her work bench, pretending to work, and glanced over at the blighted patch of carpet, testing to see if the distance made it any more tolerable. It did not. I cannot work with a view of that, she thought. She went into the downstairs hall bathroom and brought out a little oval-shaped rug that was in front of the toilet. She walked back and pitched it on top of the rose remnants. The little rug, flamingo pink and smelling of cleanser, was ridiculous situated in the middle of the carpeting, almost harder to ignore than the pieces of the petals. Exasperated, she left the lab, slamming the door behind her.

For several days, she sat down at a bench to continue work on the thornless rose, only to find that she could not work. It was as if she was being distracted by an invisible hand, tugging at her, summoning her back to the patch of carpet covered by the little rug. With each failed attempt at resuming her efforts, she became more and more aggravated. Finally one night she decided to do something about the carpeting. She moved her work bench and chair, the throw rug and other stuff aside, and began pulling up the carpeting and pad beneath it. It was slow going by herself, but eventually it was up and she put everything back where it belonged on the concrete floor. She rolled up the carpeting and pad as best she could and put them in the greenhouse. The exertion felt good and she went to bed tired but satisfied that she could come back to her work the next day with a clean slate.

The following day was no more productive, however. Whatever she started on once she returned home from the university was punctuated by a question mark. Should she review her process more carefully? Was the greenhouse too hot or too cold? Was the rose the wrong flower to start with? She could not recall such futility before, and she knew she could not bring herself to tell anyone about it. Just to talk about it in the abstract, much less go into her work in detail and then say anything about the blackened petals in the carpeting, was beyond her. She could see her dream of wealth and independence receding into the distance. The fall semester was coming to a close, with papers and finals to grade; winter break approached, when her daughter would be at home with her friends calling and showing up at all hours; the spring term brought a new department commitment advising students that would further cut into her free time. She wondered if her entrepreneurial plans were really a mid-life crisis in disguise, a brief fling away from the university's dreary, suffocating embrace. In retrospect her flower business plans seemed implausible, even laughable.

While she sat at her work bench the picture of walking through the campus rose garden many months earlier came to her, when she cut her finger on the thorn picking up student papers. She felt like she was being pricked a second time, but only after so much time and trouble had been spent, and such high hopes had been dashed. Part of her mind began to make plans to sell off equipment and convert the lab back into a garage. Another part became reacquainted with her aversion to roses; she couldn't believe she had let herself get involved with them. She swung her chair around in front of a file cabinet to retrieve a file with equipment purchase receipts, to check what she had paid and what portion she might recoup. The front of the top drawer had a photo of bountiful primroses taped to it; she delicately peeled it off, carried it by one corner to the kitchen sink and flushed it down the drain with the disposal running. She smiled at the pleasure she could have at repeating the procedure with the rose plants in her greenhouse, but perhaps with her neighbor's wood chipper. With that image still vivid in her mind, she went back into the lab and walked straight into the barren rose still hanging from the ceiling. The rose head now pointed straight at the floor, the string somehow caught on the stem where it had been clipped. She hadn't seen it, and it was low enough to bump her left eye as she passed. She ripped the string off the beam it was looped around and grabbed the dried-out stem, which could have snapped like a twig in her grip but only bent and twisted like a vine, adding to her frustration – rose the deceiver, the tantalizer, the destroyer of dreams. She flung the stem onto the floor and smashed it under her foot until it flattened onto the concrete, shouting, "Fuck you, rose, fuck you, fuck you!"

On a nearby bag of fertilizer were the clippers – she took them to the greenhouse and decapitated all the rose plants she could find. When that wasn't enough she uprooted all the rose canes and threw everything in a garbage bag. She was breathing heavily and surveying the room for any survivors when her vision fell on the carpet roll propped up in the corner. She pulled it back into the lab and cut the twine that had tied it up. She laid the carpet down and unrolled it until the black pieces of rose in the pile were uncovered. She grasped the clippers firmly and stabbed the carpeting, piercing it. Using both hands she strained to cut around one cluster of petal remnants, and then another, laboriously working her way counterclockwise around the carpet. Sweating and cursing to herself she kept at it until she met up with where she had started and was able to lift out the offending section of carpeting and place it on the lab bench.

Her hands ached as she put down the clippers and stared at what she had removed. It was about three feet across, made up of a series of looping arcs where she had cut around the outermost remnants of the petals: a circle comprised of little semi-circles. It was painfully clear to her, though, what the shape of the cut-out resembled. A rose bloom. She could not believe her eyes. But the shape was indisputable. God, another rose! She looked down in disbelief at the clippers that had done the cutting, and the aching hands that had guided them. Then she turned back to the carpet section, with its petal remnants stuck here and there within the outline of a rose bloom. No! she screamed, hammering at the carpeting with her fists, tearing at it to rid it of the black, shriveled pieces. She ground her teeth as her fingers worked, steadfastly, time out of mind, and when she had a small success she trumpeted her victory, exclaiming, Got you! But the carpet pile she was clawing at carried a dark stain from the remnants, so that removing material did not remove traces of their existence, and as she saw this she felt exasperated and then defeated. There would be no obliterating all vestiges of the blackened rose. She noticed the cut-out section of carpet was wet in several places – she had not realized she had been crying. Her head dropped down in despair and a deep, heaving cry, of a kind she could not remember since childhood, escaped her lips with her cheek flush against the rough surface of the carpeting.

After many minutes she got up, shuffled into the kitchen, exhausted, and went through the familiar action of making a cup of coffee. The smell of spooning the grounds into the filter, the steam rising and disappearing from the freshly poured water, the motion of stirring the cup with a spoon – all were comforting to her. She sat at her kitchen table and sipped, feeling spent and oddly peaceful. It seemed to her she had nothing to do but drink the coffee she had made. When she finished, she placed the empty cup on the counter, and walked aimlessly into the hall. The house was quiet, which she typically didn't like but was appealing to her now. The door to the lab was open, and from her vantage point she could see the carpet section – it was partially hanging over the edge of the bench where she'd left it, but shadow and light made it look folded over the edge, like a clock in a Dali painting, more pliable than it possibly could be. She found herself walking back into the lab to look at the carpet section more closely. The illusion that it was pliable vanished but her curiosity did not. She picked the carpet section up, looked at it, turned it over, and scraped at a place on the backing with her clippers. She removed the wipe board that was hanging near her work bench and maneuvered the carpet section on the same hook until the place on the backing caught. She stepped back. The more she looked at the carpet section, the more she could not turn away. The strangeness of cutting out a rose shape without realizing it struck her full force. It was incredible, what her hands had done, while ostensibly clipping around the pieces of fallen petals. How could I have not been aware at the time? she thought. How could this happen? She expanded her locus of attention to the carpet piece in its entirety, seeing it with different eyes, so that what remained stuck in the carpet pile became detached from her need to get rid of it and was now part of a mystery – a larger, inscrutable object. She looked at it as if a secret was hiding in plain sight, like a connect-the-dots drawing she could not quite make out. Briefly, a voice counseled and distracted her, saying, Your mind is playing tricks on you. This is merely a ruined piece of carpet. But the voice went silent as something else took hold, bringing her back to the mysterious image she could not quite make out, and her urge to see it in greater detail.

She went upstairs into her daughter's room, where she had not been for a long time, and pulled a chair into the closet. She grabbed the pull string for the overhead light and turned it on, dodging the chain while she stood on the chair and looked at the assortment of old clothes, toys, and keepsakes on the shelves. Their familiarity and the memories they evoked were inviting, but it did not deter her from sifting through them until she came to a box marked "Crafts" that she lifted off a shelf and put down on the floor. Inside was a mishmash of crayons, crepe paper, pipe cleaners, and many other things. She found one tiny paint brush, the kind that came with children's watercolor kits, and held on to it. She could not find the paints that came with it, but did find an old glass inkwell that her father had given to his granddaughter. She grabbed the bottom, the size of a small door knob, and turned it one direction, then another; miraculously, the inkwell was sealed tight by its stopper and still held liquid ink. She took it and the paint brush back to the lab.

Holding the ink well in one hand and the brush in the other, she sat down on a chair on rollers and moved close to the carpet section hanging on the wall where the wipe board had been. She unstopped the ink well; it was narrow at the top, but the brush fit easily inside the opening. The bristles came out a deep, rich color – blue or black, she could not tell. She held the brush carefully over the ink well while looking at the carpet. The image she could not quite see was still there, concealed within the cut-out shape of the rose. The brush went toward and then around one of the stuck petals in the carpet, leaving a patchy line of ink in its wake. She kept dipping the brush in the inkwell and painting around the petal remnants until the ink was gone, repeating the steps faithfully and diligently without thinking anything about it. She recognized how happy she was doing this, and also found the results interesting looking, unusual and artful at the same time. She had done so little art in her life, the fact that she had painted the carpet section seemed almost as remarkable as how she had cut it. The mystery of the image, the design just hidden from view, was no clearer to her, however. She decided to let it sit for the time being and go wash her ink-stained fingers. It was long past midnight, she had three classes to teach the following day, so she cleaned up and went to bed, dropping off instantly.

She returned to the lab the following afternoon, not out of interest in flower-making work but because she was curious how the rose cut-out and her ink markings would look a day later. As she turned on the lights and walked toward the carpet section she flinched and caught her breath. All the dark, sticky pieces of the rose, the focus of so much angst and fury, had fallen off the cut-out onto the floor below. She bent down and touched them – they seemed soft and warmer than was possible spread against the cold concrete. She gathered all the pieces, sitting down and jiggling them around in her hands as she did, feeling neither surprised nor upset, which she did not understand but simply accepted. She looked up and, studying the carpet section for the first time since she'd come into the lab, beheld another marvel: With the rose remnants gone, the cut-out had transformed into a painting that, for all its improbability, was unmistakable: It was a painting of thorns. She closed her eyes and shook her head to be sure it was not an apparition, but as she once again gazed into the section of carpet the likeness was all the more convincing. Somehow adding the paint-brushed ink and subtracting the shriveled rose petals had brought forth figures of thorns: sharp and smooth, rounded and jagged, pale in places and deep with pigment in others. Each seemed to have its own character, slightly different in shape or shade, with only a hint of the stem upon which it grew. They were strange yet gorgeous, and abundant: a flowering of thorns! Laughing and tearing up, sitting on the floor, she could not describe what she felt, like she was experiencing an uncharted emotion. The painting was preposterous and fabulous, fascinating and astonishing, and, as she sat and stared at it further, utterly satisfying, considering this was the hidden image she could not fathom, which the ink had teased out and the petals had obscured: What she had most wanted to purge was what she had most wanted to see.

Since she had destroyed all the roses in her greenhouse, she had to leave her house to see a living rose – such was the strength of her desire to look at and hold real thorns. She could not think where to go except back to the university. It was twilight by the time she reached the quadrangle where the rose garden was; the quaint lanterns that lit campus at night had not yet come on. It was chilly and still, and, except for the footfalls of a few solitary students passing by, silent. The luxurious scent of roses seasoned the air. She entered the garden by one of its dirt pathways. She looked for the thorniest rose plant she could find. At the opposite end of the garden from where she had started she came upon the place where a gardener had been pruning. Trimmed rose branches crisscrossed the path, near an old wheelbarrow already filled with them. She knelt down and gently cradled a few; they were robust and rippling with sharp thorns. She carefully took a hold of the longest one and carried it back to her car.

At home, she sat down on the living room couch where she had pulled apart the rose bloom some time ago. With all the room lights on she could see the thorns clearly – little neighboring witches' hats on the green surface of the stem. She lightly dragged the tips across her palm. They did not hurt, but they were very sharp; she could trace where they had gone by the thin white trails they made in her skin. Even the longest and most slender of them did not break off. A few were lighter in tone than the others – they had a weaker grip on the stem as she pushed the tips to one side. They would not stay on a rose cane forever; they would decompose just as the petals would, and the sadness and beauty of that impermanence came over her.

She went to the kitchen to look under the sink for any wood finishes or waxes she had. Then she went to the downstairs and upstairs bathrooms and grabbed what hand lotions, ointments and salves she could find. She brought all of them along with the rose branch to the lab, where she had a small store of soil amendments. For several hours she freely mixed and measured and experimented, and when she was through she reached into the bottom of a beaker and extracted a fingerful of a slick, syrupy substance. She rubbed it over and around the thorns on each stem. She knew she was nourishing them, but what she loved was how they glistened – shining strands of light into the recesses of her house – and how they smelled – summoning pungent forests of growth and decay that were far away, and right here with her.

It was late. She did not feel tired, only content. The stem with its tended thorns rested in her hands. Her mind roamed from plants she has seen to plants she had only imagined. What is my dream? she asked herself. She had no will to answer or wonder what the question meant. In her silence, she fell asleep. All the thorns on the stem slowly grew before her eyes into thin elegant candles. She finds a match in her hand with which to light them. The candles circle the rose bloom in a beautiful light. She reaches down to cup the wax that begins to drip from the candles. As she catches the liquid she finds it isn't hot -- it is cool, and smells of roses. She brings her hands together and drinks the liquid. She feels it move through her body until it reaches her heart. There she feels a rose take root and flower. She awakens and cradles the rose branch she has tended. The thorns do not hurt even as she presses them to her breast.

THE COVETER

In a time long ago, a young boy on a family trip to the Southwest wandered away from his parents to look at figures on the face of a rock. Even though they looked very old, he was captivated by how lively they were – they also had a vague resemblance to the crayon drawings he did sitting around the house or riding in the car. An old woman came up to the boy and told him the carving on the stone showed an ancient people eating honey. She said the people ate honey to honor bears, who stole honey from beehives. Bears were powerful gods and honey was food of the gods, she said. The people believed if they ate the honey it would lead to a magical bee being born in their stomachs.

The old woman took the boy by the hand and pointed to another figure where she said the bee flew around in the belly of a person. The boy was amazed – he would not have guessed this was what the carving showed. He wondered what it would be like to have a bee inside you. As if she had read the boy's mind, the old woman explained the bee could sting people if it wanted, but that was not its purpose. Its purpose was to deliver honey to parts of the body that needed healing.

At this point, the boy spoke: Do you have to steal honey from a beehive to get a magic bee? The old woman replied there are many kinds of beehives. Then the boy asked: Can you tell if someone has a magic bee? The woman replied that if you are lucky enough to have a bee, you can speak to it by running your hand in a circle on your belly. The boy looked intently at the old woman, waiting to see if she would rub her own belly. But then the boy's parents found him and descended upon him with hugs and admonitions about wandering off in the company of strangers.

Before they led him away, the boy was able to turn one last time toward the old woman and ask, in a voice the woman could hear but his parents could not, When do the magical bees sting you? The old woman replied when you take away their honey.

The boy grew into a man with a job, wife and family. His job was writing and administering grants for a large hospital. He had known nothing about the world of grants when he applied for the job right out of college – as time went on, he found out the hospital had not gotten any candidates who did know, and took the person who appeared most willing to learn. He had gradually learned to research things, and knew quite a bit about libraries, working in a small county branch library as a teenager. Before his interview, he drove to a city library and found two books on grants and two on hospitals. When he went for his interview he referenced what he'd read, and he guessed his initiative was what convinced them, among all the unqualified applicants, that he could do the job. He hadn't expected to keep the job very long, but it didn't work out that way: The pay was good, the benefits solid, and the longer he was there the more sense it made to stay.

His office was located on the first floor of a sprawling building complex. It was uninviting -- a numbered door in the middle of a long corridor – yet because he left his door unlocked, befuddled visitors or patients would sometimes come in and ask directions, a practice he heard was rare in other parts of the building. Something brought them to his door, so maybe his office wasn't anonymous. He expected to find the situation annoying, but that did not turn out to be true. He enjoyed sending people in the right direction. He knew how to direct people to all the departments in the hospital because he often walked around the hospital at lunch. A few staff located near the check-in desk locked their office doors, but when he tried it he found the practice distracting – footsteps stop, the hand briefly turns the locked door knob… it halted his work as he wondered: Who was outside, and what did he or she need? Rather than allow these questions to flower into idle speculation, he would get up and see if someone on the other side of the door needed his assistance, much as a Good Samaritan pulls off the road to help someone before devoting any thought to who the person might be. He cared for other people, and at the same time he liked to keep his inquisitive mind in check as he went about his work.

Despite the interruptions, he took pride in staying on task each day and giving the company the eight hours they paid him for. He could count on two hands how many times he had extended his lunch much beyond one hour, or come in substantially late. The vice president who he reported to always had glowing things to say about his work habits on his annual performance evaluation. Though it sounded corny when he thought about it, he did feel a sense of duty in performing his job, and was proud of his ability to work without someone looking over his shoulder. While he did not consider himself a loner, and enjoyed the company of family, friends and coworkers, he greatly appreciated having a private office and being able to work independently. When he arrived in the morning he laid out that day's schedule and to-do list, and while he would never tell this to anyone, the act of crossing off each completed task on his list was one of the highlights of his day.

But he was not a workaholic, and in fact disliked people who lived only to work. He had a cousin who missed his sister's wedding because he had a joined a new law firm and was said to be preparing for a trial, and despite some people accepting and even admiring his cousin's choice, he found it indefensible. On alternate workday mornings he ran four miles before breakfast, on a circuitous route around his neighborhood he'd mapped out himself, and liked competing in distance races – he got to know the other runners in their thirties who ran respectable times, and occasionally met some of them after races for a meal. He was intrigued by astronomy and volunteered once a month at a community telescope in the upper reaches of a nearby town, showing people how to use the eyepiece and identify what they were looking at in the sky. As befitting his old library job, he preferred to read rather than watch television and had finished a long parade of biographies and histories, his favorite topics. Over time, due to bits and pieces of lunchtime conversations at the hospital cafeteria, his reading interests became known, so that one day a member of the hospital's board of directors came into his office to ask what he should read before an upcoming European vacation.

Without question, though, family was far and away the chief focus in his life. He had frequently visited and helped his parents as they grew older; he had always been close with his younger brother, and as they aged the connection strengthened. His own family's story began with him meeting his wife at the small college they both attended. She was the first in her family to go on to college, while it was a foregone conclusion for him. After high school he had grown into a nice-looking man, but he found dating awkward and what was left unsaid at the end of the evening anxiety-producing. Women who more or less pursued him were the source of this discomfort for his freshman and sophomore years. Once he had a bit more confidence, he was able to ask out his future wife, who was enrolled along with him in a biology class. They were fatefully paired together as the class captured and identified butterflies. Both of them were introverts without much to say until he proved surprisingly capable of manipulating the net to snare specimens. She had a wary eye toward life – contemplating and preparing for when her good fortune might end – but as he snagged several butterflies in succession, a wisp of a smile shaped her lips, and he was immediately drawn to her. It was easy to ask her out and spend time with her. She was quiet, didn't fill in the gaps in conversation, allowed him to choose things for them to do, yet was possessed of a practicality and shrewdness that he increasingly marveled at, being fairly gifted in those areas himself. None of the women he had dated had established a solid credit rating by paying off a small loan, or knew a cross-town route where all the stoplights were timed; they were headstrong and manipulative with people, yet wildly unmindful of how the world worked – his future wife's opposite, really. She was clear about her future – get a good job, have children – which didn't scare him off and in fact reassured him: They were his own, unexpressed, wishes. Her slender, yet strong frame, and the short, simple cut of her dark hair, was practical and pleasing at the same time.

After marriage they waited until she was established with an accounting firm before trying in earnest to have a baby. A few years later she was pregnant with their first and only child, a boy. While it disturbed them that they were not able to conceive again, neither wanted to undergo the testing and doctor's visits necessary to find out why. This one area of their life together was not approached with calm appraisals and pieces of paper bisected with lists of pros and cons. They were happy with their son, and she was able to juggle flexible work hours and day care. They bought a three-bedroom, two-bath tract home in a new subdivision in a well-rated school district not far from her office – it was a long commute for him to the hospital, but he preferred to be the one to do the driving. He listened to news on the radio, or books on tape, and that took up the time.

Weekends were occupied easily with errands, home maintenance and family outings. Both had grown up attending church, but he was too much of a realist to abide the preaching and praying, and she did not object. If she had wished to go by herself with their son, he would not have tried to talk her out of it; he did not pass judgment on people who wanted what churches had to offer. Sometimes people, and particularly children, asked him cosmological questions while he helped them use the community telescope: What caused the explosion that created the universe? What existed before then? While these were not the exact questions people brought to church, he thought they were the same questions they did bring. He saw how confounding and disturbing the universe was, and how much people needed help with its mysteries. Since no definitive answers were coming in any of their lifetimes, religion was a useful construct, and the idea of God would suffice until the forces at work in the world were explained in the distant future. Disputing other's belief systems was foolish, when his own could not provide what they wished to know. It was also uncomfortable for him, because philosophical discussions like these, like the speculation about strangers who came to his office door, led him to ponder the unpredictability of people, which reminded him that somewhere inside he had his own, unpredictable self. He hated to receive that reminder any more than was absolutely necessary.

As years passed he was seen as a good citizen, a contributing member of society, a bread-earner with obligations and responsibilities to attend to, and willingly so. It did not bother him to talk about mortgages or car payments or lay-away plans – these were part of the fabric of how life should be for an adult. Trimming hedges, replacing faucet washers, attending PTA meetings… he treated such things as productive and practical parts of the week.

His embrace of conventionality was not stereotypical. He was not a wimpish harried husband or a cipher-faced commuter in a charcoal suit. He was athletic, good looking, intellectually curious and self-assured in a modest way. He was no one's poster boy for suburbia, corporate life, middle-class values or middle of the road politics. He managed to vary enough in every respect to avoid being categorized. No one he knew singled him out out of pity, envy or even disdain. He was not invisible, just unregarded. He happily, but not zealously, accepted his yoke of job and family — zealousness would have brought attention to him.

But over time he realized his life had one very special, very painful, quality: He ached with love for his younger brother's wife. She was a delightful, energetic, compassionate and appealing — no, charismatic — woman, and try as he might, he could not find fault with her or fall out of love with her. At the same time, he could not act on his feelings. More than just his brother's wife, she was a wonderful aunt and in-law, and was quite close to everyone in his family — in fact he felt his own young son could very easily be in love with her as well.

She had lovely thick light brown hair, worn always at shoulder length and parted in the middle as a schoolgirl would. She said it was easy that way — she was not partial to make-up and dressing up, though on special occasions, she would surprise his brother with a wild outfit found at a thrift store. She also sang for fun in an a capella women's quartet, and they sometimes performed their songs in various get-ups. She took the low parts in the harmony, tucking her chin as she strove to reach them; her speaking voice was in the low range for a woman, rich and full of timbre. She had bright, round, hazel-colored eyes and a wide mouth with nice white teeth — these were her features he had noticed first, and had gathered him in. In her style, she had a simplicity about her that made him think of preppie kids — untucked turtlenecks, old jeans, deck shoes without socks — yet she had grown up the oldest of five in a Catholic household in the Midwest. She was fairly tall, narrow waist, small breasts, slender through her legs to her bottom, though with childbirth her thighs and stomach had grown a bit heavier. She was unassuming yet naturally extraverted. She did not love to hear the sound of her own voice, yet she could interrupt any proceeding if she felt an injustice being done or a vital question being left unanswered. She was wickedly funny at times and could tell bawdy jokes in a way that offended no one. She never seemed thrown off-kilter; even deep in sorrow, as when her mother died, it seemed like the exact right time to be weeping and fasting. Like the typical eldest daughter of a working-class family, she knew how to sew a dress or apply a poultice to a bee-stung hand, but only revealed such abilities when needed; she was not interested in so-called women's work, and was usually several steps behind the laundry and dishes in her house without regret, since what she had chosen to do instead of those things were what gave her life pleasure and meaning.

He remembered the day his brother had introduced them as clearly as any day of his life. He had been Christmas shopping alone on a Saturday afternoon and had bumped into them in a crowded, festively decorated department store. His brother was so anxious to present her to him, after many gushing remarks about a new girlfriend over the phone, that he tripped over the words needed for a simple introduction. Such stumbling by his brother might have otherwise struck him as comical, but the flubs, as well as the praise, made sense when he met her – he felt, as she smiled broadly and gripped his hand and said how much she had looked forward to meeting him, that no one in the world meant as much to her as he did at that moment. She cocked her head and scrunched her nose, trying to remember a possible mutual friend; she gathered her hair with both hands into a ponytail and pulled it out from the collar of her parka, where it had bunched up; she remembered his wife's name and asked about her; she joked about a teddy bear she'd just bought on impulse, and when his brother rolled his eyes she gave him a firm, good-natured, boyish shove. Every move she made was utterly charming to him, as if he had never seen anyone doing such things before. There was no question she and his brother were already deeply in love, and so his approval meant a great deal to her; and yet, when she looked at him with her beautiful smile, he did not care why she smiled at him, much less did he care where he was, or what he had been doing a few minutes earlier. For an instant her presence wiped the world clean, and it wasn't until they had said their goodbyes that he was able to pick up his packages, take a deep breath, and continue on his shopping errand. Walking away, however, he could not stop himself from turning and looking back to where he had stood, feeling like he had perhaps lost something. Checking his pockets, going through every bag, he dimly knew it was not some item he was looking for; instead, it was her, or the feeling of being with her, that he'd left behind. It made no sense, to feel such a loss after a brief encounter in a department store, but he knew it was true.

Once he got home he bypassed speaking with his wife, who held their infant son on the living room couch, and went directly to their bedroom. Soon he was out of his clothes and taking a hot shower, soaping and scrubbing himself to within an inch of his life. He felt like a switch had been flipped, and now it was not what he had left behind, but what he had acquired, that would not let him be. He had put away his wallet, his spare change, his checkbook, his car keys, and hid the Christmas gifts and packages behind his sweaters in the bedroom closet; by all accounts he had what he had left with and what he had gone to buy, and was back amongst everything he required in life. But it was not quite adding up, and, on the chance that her fresh scent lingered on him, or that washing would have some deeper effect, he plunged into scrubbing himself under the hot shower water, hoping to emerge the man he had been at the start of the day. It was not to be.

Never-the-less, surrounded by the things of his daily world, greeted in the bedroom by his young family, he coped with what had come into him. He pushed it aside and did everything he would have normally done on a Saturday evening. His son had an unusually up-and-down night, waking up repeatedly and needing feedings, so he had a concrete reason for not sleeping well himself. The following day he filled with chores and activities, and there were brief periods during which he did not think about meeting her, or was not aware of how he had changed after meeting her. With each day, those periods increased. Time heals wounds, he told himself, treating her smile like a dagger, feeling a safer distance from what had cut into him. The idea that his wound included something which would not go away with the passing days, that a dagger remained and sank further into him, he also avoided thinking about. But it was worth it to have the space to live and think unburdened thoughts. Mainly in dreams, where he drove to work past things calling to him he dared not look at, did he relive the bargain he had made in order to continue his life the way it had been.

At first he avoided his brother's girlfriend, who quickly became a fiancé. But as close as he was to his brother, this would not work, and so he grew accustomed to occasionally seeing her, and steeling himself before the visits. When they were together, his greetings and comments were sincere but perfunctory, his eyes averted whenever possible. The experience neither reduced her appeal nor increased his well-being. He simply tried to hold everything in place inside himself, and maintain the status quo. Since he had no illusions about adulthood, he treated the occasions like other onerous duties that came up in the course of having a job, home and family. The difference was, he could take some small measure of satisfaction clearing the moldering leaves from the gutters; he did not feel that as he endured each interaction with her.

As his brother's wedding approached, he dreaded the time when eyes would be on him, the best man. He did not at any cost want to detract from an otherwise joyous occasion. He worked a long time on his toast for the reception, so that the tone and words would be honest, respectful and congratulatory, without betraying his anguish, or, even worse, his suppressed longing for the bride. Not confident expressing feelings under any circumstances, he could not imagine allowing himself emotion at such a moment; it seemed potentially ruinous. He practiced and revised the toast until he was satisfied with it. As for the other ritualistic steps to the wedding, he went over his role many times in his mind until he was sure he could do what was required of him. A proud elder brother he would be, to any who looked his way.

The day before the ceremony, though, he found his inner turmoil hard to contain. During the church rehearsal, his brother turned to him and quietly asked if he was finding the minister's instructions hard to follow. Ordinarily, he would have assumed his brother was joking – there was nothing complicated about the ceremony, and if anything he would have been the one to grasp it quickly, and come to the aid of his less mature little brother; these were parts they had played many times growing up. But he realized his brother was sincere, and that he was acting a bit lost, and grim-faced at that. He apologized for being distracted, blaming it on an unrelated matter. He smiled and put his arm around his brother, putting an end to his brother's concern. But his own worries were not so easily assuaged. At the rehearsal dinner, he drank several glasses of wine to dull his thoughts and lighten his mood.

The combined families were in high spirits; that helped him to forget his troubles and blend in.

Toward the end of the evening, as people were preparing to leave the restaurant where they had held the dinner, his brother's fiancé abruptly pulled up a chair next to his own. With a sisterly look of concern on her face, she asked if he was doing alright – perhaps his mood had been more noticeable than he thought. He said he was fine. She moved in close to him and told him how thrilled she was to soon be part of his family. He did not avoid her gaze in such close quarters; his eyes met hers – she looked ecstatic. Without speaking again she leaned in and put her arms around him, and he reciprocated. Her soft, full hair was against his cheek. He smelled basil from her dinner, mixed with a scent of her own – jasmine, he would decide later. She squeezed, and he squeezed back. He felt like something silent and delicious spilled open, as if he had had an orgasm inside of himself.

The next day, at the wedding and at the reception, and the following day, at a breakfast before the couple went off to their honeymoon, there would be more embraces, and kisses on the cheek, plus one kiss he initiated, on the mouth; her approach to him at the dinner, on the eve of marriage, made it seem safe to silently relish such opportunities to be near her. As brother-in-law, he would have such moments; why not take the pleasure they offered, even if nothing more might be in the offing? Socially appropriate times to abandon himself to his desire: It was perverse, but he could not resist. By the end of the wedding weekend, it was like she was another religion he did not believe but would not pass judgment on; another blind spot in an otherwise well-reasoned world.

After the wedding, his life would accommodate a periodic dose of intense gratification left unexplained. He would portage from visit to visit, carrying the hugs and kisses around in his memory. The hardening of himself that had once preceded each meeting with her now shifted to the days that followed. Months that became years made him practiced in the art of momentary joy followed by efforts to control and compartmentalize what had occurred. He still found satisfaction in his daily existence, still cared for his wife and son deeply, still brought a craftsman's eye to his desk every working day. Tedious jobs around the house and office did not seem any more tedious, needy people at the hospital or down his street did not seem any more needy. But somewhere inside himself he secretly, shamelessly relished his chances to be near his sister-in-law. She was the hidden reason he liked to walk around the hospital at noon; she occasionally had lunch there with a nurse friend at her station. He laid out his jogging route past the elementary school where her daughter attended, though only twice had their paths crossed and were waves exchanged. Despite his motivation, he did not really think through many of his actions, such as when to visit her and his brother's house, or how long he should hold her when hugging goodbye – they were determined at a lower level of consciousness, and he preferred to be left in the dark that way.

As much as he wanted stability for himself over the long haul, even in his desire for her, things would not remain the same. When his son was old enough to swim well, and just before his brother and sister-in-law became pregnant with their daughter, the five of them went on a three-day rafting trip. Naturally, he looked forward to it. The first day on the river, however, a rainstorm suddenly blew over. The wind came in gales and the rain made it hard to see. Perhaps he was preoccupied with making sure his wife and son were holding on tightly; as their guide tried to steer them toward the shore through the choppy water, he was bounced out of the raft and into the river. Though he was a fine swimmer, he became disoriented in a cold, grey, swirling world. Down he went. He did not know why his life jacket did not bring him to the surface. No more than ten seconds could have elapsed, yet his lungs were bursting. His arms could not propel his body through the water. Why was he stuck? Then he felt himself jerked to the surface. It was her. The current carried them downstream until they could grab a snagged branch, and wait for the guides to retrieve them. His foot had gotten wedged between two rocks; she had dived in to pull him out, and save his life.

The families and guides reconvened on a somewhat sheltered spot by the riverbank, and everyone in turn praised her for her bravery. But as grateful as he was, for the rest of that day he once again, as was the case when he was younger, could not look at her, much less hug her. He wished mightily for the roles to have been reversed. It was more than simply his male pride being punctured; he felt indebted, with no means to make the repayment. The hug or peck on the cheek he usually looked forward to would not do.

At a campfire that evening, with the storm gone and the group giddy in the knowledge that no harm had come to them, she led them in a series of camp songs as only she could do – full-throated, animated, unabashedly making up lyrics on the fly when the real ones wouldn't come to mind. During a lull, his young son, more outgoing than he normally was and wanting to contribute, started up "Clementine." He did not realize the song was about a drowning, knowing it only from many childhood sing-a-longs, and so the adults did not stop him or dwell in the irony as they joined in.

As his son soloed on the words "ruby lips upon the water," and as the group chimed in on the refrain "you are lost and gone forever...", he glanced over at his brother's wife, on the other side of the fire; she was smiling, enjoying singing the lilting old tune, but at that very second she looked at him as well. Was this a coincidence? Saviors and their saved, he had heard, sometimes became connected to each other through their experience. Her eyes seemed to hold a knowingness about him he had not seen before. It could have been the way the flickering campfire etched her face, creating mystery where it did not belong. But his explanation felt meager. He did not believe in fate, but he wondered about the power of extreme circumstances, creating connections between people, lives circling each other, then overlapping. The two of them could have some kind of bond as a result of the incident, he felt fairly sure. It did not make him think they might leave their spouses and go off together; but it added weight to their relationship that had not been there before. However mysterious it was, and however much it affected him without knowing how it affected her, he felt it later freighted the hellos and goodbyes they shared with new meaning.

His near-drowning and subsequent rescue had even more of an impact on his son. He was focused at first on the alarming possibility that his father could die. Out of the blue he would bring up the incident, checking over the details, seeing how it could have happened, and how it could be prevented in the future. As he grew older, though, his attention was more with his aunt, and her courageous act. She, and not any of the rest of them, even the well-trained guides, had saved his father's life. How lucky they had been to have her there! With each recitation of the rescue story, her virtues and capabilities grew until she could do no wrong in his son's eyes. By the time he was a teen, she was exempt from any sullen looks or caustic remarks that otherwise characterized his puberty.

While picking up his son's school notebook off the living room floor one night, he noticed a portrait sketched in the midst of his class notes.

The drawing was unmistakably of her. The full hair and wide mouth were just right, born of many erasures and second tries, and certainly at the expense of whatever lesson was being taught that day. He was not surprised his son could have a crush on his aunt – he had seen it coming. He was not angry, or despairing, or jealous; to the contrary, he was because of this more forgiving toward his son and his teenage moods, having some insight himself into what unrequited love felt like. But more than that, carrying the notebook to his son's room, he realized he must be careful to hide his own feelings. He could not leave signs of his own heartache lying around for his son or his wife to find.

Whether at work or at home, he relied heavily on his ability to organize his life, following routines and breaking them down into their component parts, creating discipline where none had previously existed. He had read the biography of a mathematician who said, when a mathematician wants to relax, he does mathematics; in his idle moments, he looked for more ways he could get from A to Z in a series of manageable steps. He even had a dream where he was writing lists as fast as he could, and dropping them into a well, to soak up the rising water. He did not want the water level to rise, though he did not know why. Since his excessive planning was an extension of the way he had always been, he felt sure no one thought much about it. He did not think he could stop managing his activities, because the instant he stopped, he would be left with that part of him that could not be managed. One force must be equal to another, he thought, and the force of his feelings for his brother's wife was formidable.

But in time he learned that the yearning for her never truly left him. It did not seem to matter where he was or what he did, how engrossed he was at work, or contented at home: Something palpable – the part he once thought he could partition or push aside – was always present inside of him. It had once been like the moon, gone for long stretches of day and sometimes night: out of sight, out of mind. Now the sight of it didn't matter, because its gravitational pull remained, tugging at his mind and body. He took to running every morning instead of every other, at a faster pace that eventually made him competitive with serious runners in his age bracket. He returned to the house each morning drained of energy, but aware that he had not exhausted the feeling for her that was also inside of him. He could count on running extinguishing a mood or state of mind – but not this.

When he made love to his wife, he needed only to close his eyes in the darkness to find the yearning inside of himself. Eyes open he was full of the same tenderness he had always felt for his wife; eyes closed, and the sights, smells and sounds that could not completely be associated with his wife, that could be imaginatively attached to another particular woman, were unbearably erotic. The merest ambiguity of who he was with in the dark pushed him into a sexual frenzy. But the yearning was not dissipated by any of his climaxes. And it was still there when he held his wife, quietly, in the gentle light of morning.

He began to stop by an obscure bar on his way home from the community telescope each month. Never much of a bar-going type, he was drawn to the poorly marked, dimly lit building that seemed to have a sign above the door, "To forget your troubles, enter here." But no matter how much he had to drink, the yearning was not dulled or washed away. Only the sense of refuge vanished, for once the bartender engaged him in conversation he soon lamented his unkind fate at the hands of she who would remain nameless.

Each new book he read, even those meticulously chosen to avoid any semblance of romance or sexuality, contained turns of phrases or minor themes that evoked desire, which he felt not as an abstraction, but as a touchstone. He found, and came to expect, his yearning imbedded in every story. There was no avoiding it. And that was his new reality: A yearning that would not fade. Regardless of his unrelenting efforts, now it was with him moment to moment.

Each day, he sat with it, slept with it, laughed with it, suffered with it. In time he came to be obsessed with it.

As part of his obsession, he decided the yearning had a location in his body, a place from which it emanated. He estimated the location was his abdomen. The closest he could get in describing it was an unsettled feeling, but he definitely felt it had a physical presence, and the more he focused on it, the more he wanted to seek medical help, to see if it could be removed or medicated into submission. Without telling his wife or son, he went to see several doctors. He did not discuss with them the origins of the feeling, and when they asked he answered he did not know. He knew it was a lie, but the lie added an otherworldliness to the conversation – he welcomed that, the detachment from where he had been, and he felt comfortable repeating the lie and almost fooling himself that it was true. The doctors mentioned ulcers, hernias, pulled muscles – these and other more obscure causes were considered and ruled out. When he had his stomach x-rayed, he could scarcely wait for the results. The doctors found nothing unusual, but he studied the film like a beach where someone had dropped a diamond ring. Other tests and procedures followed, all ambiguous or ineffectual. Casually, he asked a specialist if he would consider doing exploratory surgery; the response was no, but the doctor stuttered giving his reply, the request clearly unnerving him.

When there were no other doctors to see, he read up on alternative medicine and non-Western treatments. Chiropractors, acupuncturists, herbalists, body workers and others followed, all failing to do what he required. He expanded the range of possibilities. The hospital employees association, which represented many workers of Asian descent, sponsored a trip to China, and he convinced his family they needed a vacation, though they had never gone on such a far-flung, expensive trip before. Once they arrived, in a long-planned maneuver, he feigned illness the morning of a day-long trip to the Hidden City, and instead he snuck off with a guide to a what was called a medicine-less hospital. He had heard of it reading the broken English on the box of an audio tape for sale in an herbalist's office; after purchasing the tape, he listened to a barely decipherable description of a place where healers called chi-masters could extract the bad part of a person by the power of their hands. The list of illnesses recited that had been cured was extraordinary. The tape box had a photo on it of people serenely scattered on a hillside beneath a large building, which he presumed to be the hospital. They were all identically dressed in loose white pants and shirts with no discernable expressions on their faces. This was a place, he decided, where any torment or yearning could be excised from a person. After several months of inquiring with the herbalist's assistance, he had arranged the visit.

It took four hours of driving, past thousands of Chinese in urban and rural settings, on foot, on bike, in cars, impassively moving about, until the guide came to the hospital of the photo on the tape box. The hair on his neck stood up in anticipation as he and his guide were ushered by two men into the hospital and down a cool, unadorned hallway. They were led into a big but spartan room with only an examination table in it. Waste-high, the table was covered with a white sheet draped over the sides, matching the white walls and ceiling. Four others came in, and he expected the two men and his guide to withdraw – they were dressed in Western-style shirts and pants, while the four new men wore the robes from the hillside in the photo, looking exactly as he pictured them. Instead the new men motioned him over to the table and formed a wide circle around him, making a point to include the other two men and his guide. No one asked him any questions or gave him anything to read. He sat on the table, and one of the robed men motioned for him to lie flat on his back and lift his shirt, pointing and saying "ab-do-men" in halting and heavily accented English. The herbalist had written ahead, telling them where his problem was located, so they apparently knew who he was.

Without hesitation the four robed men began chanting "Fa-chi, fa-chi, fa-chi," moving rhythmically while slowly working the circle toward him. The fingers on their hands were spread, palms facing him, gently pushing against the air. After a few minutes the other two men and his guide picked up the chant and moved with the others. More minutes passed and they were close enough to touch him. The oldest robed man had a thick fringe of hair that matched his clothing: bone white in color, bouncing freely with each movement. The old man's eyes were closed tightly as he chanted and moved. The longer he looked at the old man, the more encouraged he became. Surely this aged healer had helped others in worse shape, he thought. Many people with life-threatening illnesses came to the medicine-less hospital and left feeling cured. He did not have cancer or heart disease. The old man's hair, the robe, the walls and ceiling... he could not find a speck of dark in any of them; he felt drenched in white, a healing white. This sterile room, with no hint of feminine influence, thousands of miles from home... how could his desire survive here, he thought. He listened to the chanting. The men's voices blurred and blended, until he couldn't really hear them any more. He felt happily numbed from the verbal battering. As the Chinese accents evaporated, and only sounds remained, it seemed that this barren room could be anywhere.

Shifting his head, he saw one of the other robed men looking at him intently – perhaps this was the chi-master. Moments after their eyes met, the man placed his hands on his exposed stomach. His body bounced on the table, reacting to the sudden sensation of heat from the man's hands. Almost in response, the chanting stopped. What did it mean, he thought. Was he cured? He watched as the robed men withdrew from the room, taking the others with them. His ears rang from the chanting. He pulled down his shirt. It was very quiet outside. What next? He looked at the closed door, keeping his body as still as possible, as if any movement might matter. Once he thought he heard steps stop outside the door. No one came in. He stared at the door and thought about his closed door at work, and how he often looked at it and wondered when someone was outside. He was always ready for who might be there needing help. They were lost, and he assisted them, but it was he, most assuredly, who was really lost, he thought. Because whoever came to the door, that person was not the one he secretly hoped to encounter. His job, his life, felt like a wandering. Circumscribed, methodical, but a wandering none-the-less. He imagined seeing her walk through the door at that moment. No make-up, hair a bit unkempt, but wide-eyed, smiling and flushed in the face from the excitement of travel. She circled the room and poked fun at the lack of decoration. She did a mock rendition of the Fa-chi chant, then covered her mouth and giggled, aware she might have been overheard. Turning a touch more serious, she tried to cajole him into exploring the hospital grounds; she had been reading up on chi energy, and wanted to learn more. He closed his eyes and covered his ears, until he imagined her no more. Lying alone on the table in the silence, he felt emptied and laid bare by the chi-masters. But not bereft of her; she was still there, like an essential part he was left with, one of the vital organs they could not remove. He was stripped of everything he had to keep her at bay – his distractions, illusions, machinations – and wanted her still. He felt like a marooned sailor with nothing to eat who fed on the most vivid, most alluring memories of his life.

He wanted to hold her, learn from her, laugh with her, make love to her. Here, there, or anywhere, at home or in a remote corner of the planet, he couldn't keep his mind off her. It felt futile to try.

The rest of the trip seemed uneventful and anticlimactic; he felt he had received an answer to a question, and was resigned to it as he was resigned to the stirring in the pit of his stomach. He was less agitated and distracted, and moved about in a light fog of certainty. He stayed close to his wife and son, appreciating them more than he had in weeks. He went on the tour buses and saw the new and ancient China they had read about together, grateful for how exotic and unfamiliar it was to anything he knew.

When they returned, his brother planned an evening to hear about the trip. The two families would gather for dinner and sharing of photos and stories. As he thought about seeing his brother's wife, he did not feel he could ever be stoic or subtle or shrewd anymore; he did not feel capable of anything other than where his yearning led him. One sleepless night before the gathering, it came to him that he had reached a crossroads – tell his brother's wife how he felt, or end his life. That night he paced around his room, listening to his wife's soft sleep, then went into the room of his son and watched him sleep. By daybreak he had decided he would go see his brother's wife.

He called in sick, saw his wife and son off in the morning, then drove to her house. He let himself in and found her writing at a small desk in the corner of the kitchen. His brother and their daughter had already left; no one else was home. She was wearing a pair of baggy grey sweat pants, a rust-colored corduroy shirt with the tails hanging out, and old sheepskin-lined slippers. She acknowledged him with a smile as she finished what she was doing. Before she could stand up and embrace him, he said, "I love you."

"I love you, too," she said warmly, barely glancing up from her writing.

He was elated, but knew he had not made clear what needed to be clear. "I love you more than as a sister-in-law," he said. "I love you as a man loves a woman." It sounded terribly awkward to him, but he could not think how else to put it.

She put down her pen and turned in her chair toward him. Her face was placid, body still; she looked at him with what he felt was great care. Rarely was she at a loss for words, but she was now, though that brought him no pleasure; the wait was agonizing. Finally, she said, "I don't love you in that way."

He felt as if he had been shot. He tried to remain standing, but he felt his legs give way and he went down to his knees. She stood up and moved toward him and he grasped her calves like a child trying to stand up. Tears came, the first he could remember in a very long time. He sobbed in a deep, unrecognizable voice. She put a hand on his head but did not try to lift him up from the floor. He could not look up at her. Even though he had not chosen to end his life, by choosing instead to tell her how he felt, and hearing her reply, his life seemed over none-the-less.

Then for some reason he turned his head and found himself looking through his tears at the kitchen refrigerator. There was a large child's drawing stuck to it by magnets, no doubt done by his niece, his brother and his wife's only child. It was a crayon drawing of a smiling little girl. She was surrounded by stalky green plants with purple tops, with a big yellow ball of a sun and twinkling stars shining down from the corner of the paper. The most skillful aspect by far was the way she drew a tiny winged creature flying around in the little girl's tummy. He could not take his eyes off that part of the drawing. The room, his sense of where he was, receded. Time stopped. Long ago and here and now merged. And then he remembered what he had forgotten, and it seemed so incomprehensible to him later that he had forgotten: the family trip to the Southwest, his discovery of the rock carvings, his talk with the old woman. He crawled on his hands and knees to the drawing, took it from the refrigerator, sat down cross-legged, and gently laid it in his lap. He wiped his eyes so no tear would fall onto it. His niece had drawn the bee in the belly of a person, just as he had seen in the rock carving as a boy. What was possible and what was not suddenly seemed like water from the same well. And how long would that be?

He scrambled to his feet and quickly asked his brother's wife, before any other words could be exchanged between them, if he could have the drawing to take with him, right then. She said yes. By the time he had gotten home he had remembered everything that had been said by the old woman, which took on deeper meaning with each passing second. He closed the door to his house, sat down on the sofa in the living room, closed his eyes, and placed his hand on his stomach. Nervously but eagerly he rubbed his hand in a slow circle. The feeling he felt he'd had for so long in the pit of his belly transformed and spread through his body, bringing warmth and peace and softness he had not known existed. Tears rolled down his cheeks that tasted sweet as well as salty in his mouth. It led him naturally to smile. When he felt he could speak he called his wife at work and told her he was coming to pick her up. When she asked what was going on, he said, "I've got a secret to tell you."

THE SHUNNED

Each was born apart. He came into the world with a leer, a lascivious look that undressed and unsettled people it fell upon. She began life with a grey veil between herself and everything she wanted – soft hands and faces, the smooth sheets she slept on, the warm milk from the bottle. She did not know what it was, but even though she did not feel it would last, each day she would open her eyelids and believe in a deep way that does not take thinking that the veil would finally be gone. In time she wished she had a name for it; she yearned for her parents to acknowledge it, to teach her how to make it go away, to console her about it, but none of this happened and it was the one, huge aspect of her life that lived in the shadows, as she did.

As an infant he had a look of knowingness and satisfaction, an old soul in its final incarnation, gazing contentedly over everything he had seen before. When he cried in his mother's arms to be fed or put to sleep she could predict the end of the crying by the return of the look, his essential expression – "I know you" – that returned to his face and was his primal mode of being. As his features became more distinct, the look seemed less like observing and understanding and instead a honing into people and scrutinizing them with apparent relish. "What does he know?" was the unstated response to his look, his seemingly self-satisfied, indulgent study of anyone and everyone, that, in defiance of his age and appearance, led people to imagine he wished to touch them, feel their skin, make them squirm, and even do unmentionable things he could not possibly know about and yet looked as if he did, with utter delight and abandon.

Once he was grown he was not ugly or plain-looking, nor was he handsome or exotic looking. His dark eyes stood out beside his fair complexion, and the fullness of his mouth was noticeable, but no single feature could explain what people saw in him. They looked at his expression and shuddered at the possibility he was contemplating carnal acts they thought about but did not admit to anyone. Girls would absently tug their skirts down, cross their arms over their breasts, check the top buttons of their blouses to make sure they would not come loose. At a young age he did not know why he elicited the reactions he did, and no one, not even his mother, would explain it to him. He took no pleasure in it – he was not old beyond his years, preternaturally attuned to sexuality – but it was fascinating to him none-the-less what occurred. When he looked at a girl he would silently count to ten as he watched, waiting for her to grow uneasy, or cover up a part of her body.

In time the game became joyless, because he was left alone by girls, and even though other boys would play with him, they knew he was different, and often avoided him also. It was no solace to him that other boys sometimes made girls uncomfortable; the discomfort they caused was usually slight, almost matter-of-fact, and even welcome at times, while he provoked an ever-increasing reaction until girls and later women could not tolerate his presence. They would get angry at him and complain about his staring, even when he consciously did not stare, and their fathers, brothers, boyfriends or husbands would confront him and threaten to make him pay for his impertinence unless he left. He tried to find the right words to explain that he had always affected people this way and could not avoid it, but it was futile. The frustration of making people uncomfortable and angry simply by looking at them was enormous, matched only by his confusion at not knowing why he should be different from others, to be shunned, bullied and despised for the look on his face.

She, on the other hand, wanted confrontation, but it was with an inanimate object, a mist that never lifted from in front of her eyes. When she was certain no one was around, she would pound her eyes and brow with her fists, trying to dislodge the fog or punch at least a small hole in it so she could see. Or she would bounce her head against the wall until tiny sparks would appear at the moment of impact, giving her a semblance of hope, but then her parents or other adults would arrive to stop her, ruining any chance the sparks would grow in strength. She flailed against their restraints, screamed at the low dull voices, cried out to at least fill the darkness with sound. Her rage was impossible to contain. Its intensity was pure and its purpose unambiguous. Perhaps her fury could erase the veil! But it did not.

After many, many explosions of anger she one day seemed to run out of them, like her spirit had been emptied. It may have been the day, finally, she was told about herself, by a teacher. You are blind, the teacher said. Blind. The word meant more to her than any she had learned. It was sharp, quick, painful, but real, like the cold knives in the kitchen drawers she was forbidden to touch. She felt the word strike her in the forehead and go straight through her head down the back of her spine. Blind. The shock to her body held truth; she felt weak and fragile yet closer to what she strove for than any time she could remember.

The teacher spoke about darkness – it was not beyond the understanding of others, and she was not the only one in the world who suffered from it. What do I do? she asked the teacher. You get used to it, her parents said. No one spoke after that, and as the seconds passed she felt terrifyingly alone. She tried to scream but no breath was available to her. Get used to it? How can you get used to a black cloud? She didn't care what happened to her then – life was pointless inside a fog that never lifted. A deep, deflating breath pitched her head forward, chin on chest. It was a pose that she would unconsciously take many times in her life. She slumped in a chair with only her breath as a vital sign. Her parents, unmoved by her new passivity, left her alone with her misery and isolation.

He, too, was abandoned by people, as they responded to his leer and wanted nothing to do with him. This was particularly painful in puberty, when he found he was strongly attracted to girls. When he was snubbed the pain was all the greater now wishing he could explore his new feelings with girls, and fumble his way toward intimacy like other boys. Ironically, while he could not remember ever being truly innocent, as he was a magnet for other boy's crude remarks and knowing looks – they incorrectly assumed he was sexually precocious or schooled by someone in all things licentious – he had a typical patchwork knowledge of sex. Even though he liked being mistaken for a sexually knowledgeable boy, he would have traded all of that fleeting schoolyard prestige for any real experience of his own.

Kept at a distance, he was left with a jumble of suggestive words, comments and images to fuel his incipient sexual desire. He realized the way he had always looked now betrayed his new thoughts. Girls made him excited, and his face was a window to what he felt between his legs. As he grew taller, more muscular, with facial hair and a deeper voice, reactions to him grew: Girls sometimes gasped when they saw him for the first time. Even if they had never imagined being raped, or even touched in a sexual way by a man, they were horrified by what his look portended. They felt exposed, vulnerable, abused, objectified, regarded and yet at the same time disregarded, powerful and yet powerless, unsafe, unclean, impure. They, their families and their friends singled him out in hushed voices and wanted him out of their lives. Several girls made unfounded claims against him: That he had hid in a bathroom and watched them use the toilet; that he had climbed into their rooms at night and secretly taken pictures of them while they slept; that he had reached into their clothes on a crowded bus and felt their bodies; and scenarios much more elaborate than these. When the stories circled back to him, often told by a cruel classmate getting vicarious pleasure from his predicament, he would feel gripped by a simultaneous clutch of fear and arousal. He was shaken by the knowledge that his mere presence in the world could so threaten women and create such baroque fantasies that he would not be allowed near them and might be persecuted for even looking at them.

At the same time, though it felt disastrous to his youthful sense of right and wrong, he could not help being titillated when he was alone, thinking about his ability to sexually menace women. While he dreamed of the adoring gaze of a girl who loved and cared for him, he also fantasized about the libidinous acts that were falsely attributed to him. Inhabiting the skin of the monster they thought he was brought him gratification, but regret afterwards. He did not know if all sexual urges ended this way, or if it was desire twinned with revenge that left him sad and conflicted.

He wondered if living in a different, far-off place would change his situation. He did not hold out much hope, as wherever he went, his look brought the same strong reactions. With each year his body acquired new reflex responses, like instant attempts at reparations: palms raised up at his sides; hands clasped in front of his groin; shoulders dropped or held high and tight; eyes downcast; teeth clenched or widened in a smile. None assuaged people's worries about his intentions or reduced the intensity of his leering look; eventually they fell away or became so distilled that they were unrecognizable as anything but little tics of nervousness. As a buffer against reactions and accusations, they had no impact, but he noticed over time that fewer and fewer people bothered to ask him about himself, if he was aware of the effect he had on people, and if he cared. Perhaps they knew he would have forsaken the leer by that age if he had wished to and was therefore helpless to change his appearance. In any event, he made verbal apologies less and less, as they weren't effective. He had his involuntary gestures, he avoided eye contact if possible, and for whatever reason his confrontations with people lessened.

The more separate he was, the more he craved the normal human interaction others had and he did not. Any chance at anonymity in order to experience this he leapt at. As a boy he couldn't wait to wear a mask on Halloween, though it was only a matter of time before other children guessed his real identity. When older he experimented with hats, glasses and facial hair. Once he engaged with people, however, they eventually were disturbed by him, regardless of what he did to hide his eyes, mouth or other parts of his face. How did they know? Where was his telltale mark?

Those who knew him did not need to physically see him to be discomforted; he could be on the phone or merely mentioned by name. He was not just an unwelcome presence in a room but the embodiment of lechery in the circles he moved in: the butt of a joke; the object lesson used by parent with child; the face seen by a woman in the middle of the night. His notoriety seemed impossible to erase. He did not see any way to change how he was perceived by people and avoid the unjust fate that had come upon him.

She similarly felt defeated, unable to do anything to change her situation. Her explosive behavior as a child had ended, but it still cost her her freedom. Much of the day she had been confined to her room, and later she was sent away by her parents to a boarding school for the blind where she was closely supervised despite being mostly passive or inert. She became attuned to the slightest, most insignificant objects in her time alone – a creaky floorboard, the plastic arm of a long-lost toy soldier, the nub of a pencil – and cared nothing for the lessons and socialization at the school by comparison. Her world, which she shared with no one else, was made up of the forgotten, broken and makeshift that had no value to anyone but her. Most of the children in the school ignored her, except when a kind of mass mayhem took over, where the students for a brief period gained control of the classroom screaming and running amok before the teachers joined forces to put an end to it. It did not rekindle her wild rages from before, but she enjoyed being swept up in the bedlam, the physicality of the careening bodies, the smell of sweat, the screeching sounds of terror and delight. Teachers routinely watched her to guard against self-mutilation, but in the melee she would bite her lip for the tang the blood left in her mouth – the taste of a familiar friend.

One older blind girl in the school befriended her – a husky-voiced girl that breathed heavily and slapped the walls and floor loudly finding her way around. She would be awakened by the older girl when it was at its most quiet at night. The older girl would put one hand on her forehead and one on her pelvic bone, firmly and surely, as if she could see her lying in bed, the touch rousing and restraining her at the same time. The two of them would quietly find their way to a closet off the dormitory floor, where there was a chute used for sending dirty clothes to the basement for washing. The students were forbidden to enter the closet for fear of one of them climbing into the chute, but because of steady use, sometimes it was left unlocked, and the older girl checked for this every night. So when the two of them made it to the closet door, the older girl turned the knob achingly slowly, and it gave way.

Inside the closet, they carefully positioned themselves around the mops, brooms and buckets until they could sit, arms and legs intertwined. Then the older girl pulled back on the heavy swinging door to the laundry chute and held it open. A sweet-smelling echo of air hit them in the faces, followed by what the older girl had found, and wished to initiate her friend into: the far-away word-less chants and wails of two voices. "They are doing the dirty deed," the older girl hoarsely whispered the first time they hid, which meant nothing to her other than to add this signature sound to other things that adults did which she did not like. In their subsequent nocturnal visits, though, she would imagine the voices reverberating outside the school, in the lands without walls and doors, in the open air that naturally smelled sweet, and she came to associate the sounds with freedom from restraint and guardianship. After the older girl left the school, she thought about becoming less timid and more capable of taking care of herself so she could someday be free to do what she wanted.

He was desperate to set out on his own and was frequently reminded he could do so at age eighteen by his mother, who also labored under the weight of his appearance and saw her life improving with him gone. She herself had been banished at an early age due to pregnancy, punished for a period of rebellion and sexual profligacy as a teen and told to move out and find the father of her child, which she could not do. She supported the two of them as best she could, and turned away from men and relationships with bitterness and disgust. His face to her was the vague reminder of many young and eager sexual partners she had had, one of whom was the father, who had dropped out of sight and thus free from responsibility. She hated that missing man, as well as her long-extinguished desire for him, and while she did not hate her son, he was the connection to the lost father, and what he had done. She felt responsible for her son, and would defend him from his worst accusers, but ultimately looked forward to the time when he was not around; not just because of the increase in freedom and opportunities it promised, but because the not-fully conscious awareness she had when he was around – that there was unrelenting lust in the world and it had ruined her – would be gone.

When he left he found some relief in characteristic men's work: unskilled physical labor, then construction, then any job as long as it meant he could live with some privacy. It was most tolerable for him when women were scarce and the work was hard or dangerous enough to keep everyone occupied, reducing any possible attention to his appearance. Whenever possible, though, the men talked of women constantly, often in the most coarse terms possible. When he left home he was a virgin, but just as before, there was little doubt about his worldliness on the part of others. Even the most profane men assumed he was as experienced as they were. They unquestioningly accepted his contributions to the sexual chatter, which were based on the things he knew of or had been accused of but never did, or his imaginings of what men and women did together. It did not trouble him to pass these stories off as true, because the benefits of being accepted or at least unchallenged outweighed his trafficking in falsehoods. However, at a deeper level, it bothered him a great deal, because it was a sad acknowledgment of his detachment from other people and even more so how much he wished to know a woman intimately.

As soon as he had the knowledge and money he hired a prostitute to come to his apartment. He hoped it would be someone who actually would enjoy his leering expression and perhaps match it with one of her own, and he had asked for the most experienced person the service employed. But when she arrived, she seemed as young and frail as how most women seemed to him, though she did not flinch when she looked at him and conducted the business of her fee. It was a tremendous relief when she took her clothes off and watched him take his own off, revealing his erection. She rolled a condom onto him and led him to his bed. She straddled his waist, placed his hand between her legs and guided him into her. He was afraid to move for fear of what her reaction might be to him; at the same time, he rejoiced in the agonizing pleasure of being inside her and feeling her slowly raise and lower herself on him. It lasted for several glorious minutes before he came. She stopped moving, and he lay with his eyes closed for a moment, feeling contented at finally having the experience of sex with a woman.

He hoped to open his eyes and see her looking at him. But when he looked at her, her head was turned, and she stared absently at the rug on the apartment floor. "Hello," he said, not knowing what to say. "How was that," she said, still turned away. He did not know words that could describe what he felt.

Soon she was putting her clothes on and preparing to leave. "What about another time," he said. She told him the procedure, but what he really wanted was some indication from her that it had not been torturous to be there, that she could look at him and feel at least comfortable or perchance even aroused. He could not find the strength to ask straight out, and she would not reveal more – as swiftly as she could, she left. When he called the service again and asked for her, she was not available. And then he realized how unusual she had been, for the next woman would not take all her clothes off in his presence or look at him, and the woman after that started to cry when he asked her to repeat her name, and left immediately.

In frustration he frequented strip clubs where he could mingle with other leering men, but even there the dancers seemed chastened by his appearance and less seductive when he was watching. Some took his money, but they seldom bared their bodies in front of him, and whenever the opportunity arose, they turned away and denied him what little bit of interaction there could be between them.

One night he approached the stage when a buxom dark-haired woman was dancing. She had a large frame and a more confident angle to her steps than the other dancers. He held out a large amount of money to ensure she would perform for him in return for the tip. She left the center of the stage and strode toward him, eyes fixed on the money he held out. She was at the end of her routine and had already removed everything but a G-string. Kneeling where he stood by the raised stage, she leaned forward until her thick, ringleted hair dangled in front of his face, something she no doubt did to tantalize men. Then she jerked her head up, flipping her dark hair backward in a stylized move. Her tongue coursed over her lips mechanically while she smiled and stared into the dark outer reaches of the club. She was so close to him he could see the delicate imprint her pubic hair made on the patch of cloth covering her.

When she looked down at him with her hair flipped back he could tell it was the first time she had really seen him. The big mannerisms and self-confidence evaporated and she recoiled, covering her breasts with her hands. It was all too familiar, her reaction to him and his repulsion and fascination with that, yet it was intensified by how close to each other they were. He could not move, feeling exposed and revealed in the club's stage lights. He watched her strong body loosen like an untethered puppet, and without reaching for his money she awkwardly turned away, teetering on her high heels. Part of him wanted to jump on the stage and grab her, make her look at him one more time; another part felt ashamed he was a such scourge of women.

Once she had disappeared back stage the other men's queries – "What did you say?" "What did you do?" – prompted him to quickly exit the club, never to return.

Some weeks later, there was a message on his phone at home. A woman with a calm, deep-toned voice said she regretted not finding him there, to address him in person. The woman said she had gotten his number to let him know she was a dancer he had seen at the club, and since she had looked at him one night she had not been back, and would never strip in front of men again. He knew by her account that it was the dark-haired woman. She said she believed he had been sent to her as a sign from God, and thanked him for what he had done. He clenched his fists, feeling his own sense of fate crowd around him, as she wished him well and hung up to end the recording. Am I destined to terrify women and chase them into chastity? he thought. You withheld nothing as God withheld nothing, she had said on the recording. He took his fists and pounded his head until his hands ached. I deserve to be loved, too! Where is the woman who can see past the curse of my face!

By contrast, her rage and defiance seemed so distant that she sometimes could not even conjure up a memory of herself flying across the room or banging the walls. Whatever she imagined it took to be free of the school and discover what lay outside her confinement, she did. She raised her head when spoken to, learned the minimum that was required and recounted at bedtime the things that she had done to expand her privileges. Only when she was alone and idle did the waiting weigh on her; collapsing on the floor, chin dropping to her sternum, questions without answers floating in the gauzy distance in front of her head. If it went on too long she would cover her ears and focus only on the vibrations from other rooms she felt up from her

legs and through to her pelvis. That settled her and passed the time
until the next thing came along she had to do.

She didn't mind shutting out her hearing, but she could not bear
to wear gloves or cover her legs or arms -- she enjoyed touching things,
and people, and could not part with that. She knew each person in the
school and their tolerance for touching, she knew from feeling those
faces she found interesting and those she didn't.

The small girl came to her on a day when she had her chin down
sitting cross-legged in a room by herself. She felt fast steps approach,
with reproachful voices in the distance, and then someone jumped on
her back, pushing her forward face against the floor with her legs caught
underneath her body. Little feet bounced against her back, hitting her
vertebrae like the bars of a xylophone, and then they were gone. Soon
she heard others say who this was, a small blind girl who had come into
the school and suddenly could see again. The staff was allowing her to
stay until other arrangements were made, though they spent a good deal
of time chasing her down and monitoring her activities.

Now that she was aware of this small girl who could see, she
tuned into her voice and movements whenever she could. There was
a brightness and liveliness to the small girl's movements, though they
were hard to discern amidst all the other children due to her celebrity;
the small girl was the sighted one among them and they gathered
around her continually. The small girl liked physical contact, and was
prone to bowling over the other kids when the staff was not around.
She loved this when it happened to her and she tried to place herself in
the small girl's path.

One day the small girl charged into her again: This time she was
on her feet and held her ground; instead of moving to her next target,
the small girl climbed up her body until her little legs were wrapped

around her neck. "I'll guide you," the small girl said, leaning down to whisper into her ear. The small girl told her she had sat like this many times on her father – he had been her eyes as she directed him to go one way or another. "Now I can see," the small girl said, and proceeded to grab two handfuls of hair on either side of her head to move her left or right. She was wobbly, only getting a short distance away before staff stopped them, but when they were alone they tried again and she felt steadier and she and the small girl got further. Whenever they finished she felt the heat of the small girl's thighs on her neck, and marveled how hard she could squeeze her little legs together, and wrap her tiny fists around handfuls of hair.

Parents arrived for special occasions, and on these days neither her parents nor the small girl's parents were present. Taking a chance, she called out, and while staff were distracted the small girl found her and climbed up. "Let's look outside," the small girl said softly, and she pulled her one direction after another until the sounds of the staff and other children grew more remote. Her pulse pounded as she imagined them at the far reaches of the schoolyard, at the boundary of freedom. "Step up," the small girl said, and she did, finding her footing on a ledge that allowed her to get higher and feel a cold metal surface against her forehead. She moved forward and molded her body against it. "You're looking right at it!" the small girl shouted in her ear. She heard the small girl describe what she saw while she felt the squeezing legs and grasping hands – a fullness of experience that led her to pant for air and lock her knees so they would not buckle. These descriptions of the seen world from someone who was so recently like herself, behind a veil, brought a joy that was singular and unequaled.

She knew they could not stay and would get in trouble if they did, but that did not matter; she worshipped every second. As she pressed against the fence she felt a warmth travel from the back of her neck where the small girl's legs were down through her midsection and the bottom of her stomach to the openness between her legs. She had grown taller, her shoulders and hips had widened, and her height provided the small girl with a view the others could not. In return, the small girl told her about the new world she could see.

Despairing of life and any opportunities with women, he showed less and less interest in the world and what it offered. By night he retreated into fantasy, a vivid imagining of a villain's role he secretly played, a masked man named Sweet who no woman could resist and no man could stand up to. When he needed cash, bank tellers would give him money; when he wanted to have sex, women removed their clothes and catered to him; when he needed anything, people were forced to do whatever he bade them to do. If police interfered he told them it was pointless to resist and they put down their weapons. If his voice or reputation were not enough to sway people, he would ask them to touch his costume – red cape, black pants and shirt – and they would either swoon or whimper.

No one had been able to figure out the source of his power; in fact, it was an infinitesimal quantity of anti-matter he carried with him and wore at his waist beneath his belt. Anyone within a certain distance lost the ability to resist him due to the strange properties of the anti-matter, which changed a person's body chemistry, experienced as a weakening of will. Women found it highly sensual, and men did not dislike it – hence the name, bestowed on him by the public: Sweet. People felt he was at heart a heroic figure, using the money he took for good deeds, treating women to pleasure they would otherwise never experience, and that his name was not in any way ironic, that he had a generous soul hidden away beneath his costume. But Sweet was actually not the least bit generous in spirit, and saw no reason not to use people under his sway in any way that suited him.

He lay awake imagining people serving Sweet, doing his bidding, and he could fantasize Sweet exploiting them an endless number of times. The satisfaction of complete compliance and control was intoxicating – he could lie in bed and put himself in the role of Sweet and be happier than he had ever been. During the day, he sometimes slipped into a pleasing reverie, imagining he was Sweet and could take off a special coat he wore over his costume shielding people from anti-matter effects and then they would be under his power. His fantasy time was preferable to everyday work, tasks, errands and interactions, which felt like endurance tests that he moved through laboriously, like a diver at the bottom of the sea. Nighttime was preferable, when he was by himself and could imagine things that real life could not or would not afford him.

As she grew older her solitary life receded as she finally, blessedly was able to leave the school and later reunite with the small girl in a halfway house along with other women. She received enough money from her parents for both of them to live off, and while they had to share a room with others, they spent time together alone when they could. When they were the only two in the house, or when just the two of them went out, the small girl sat on her shoulders as she had before and guided her movements and talked about what she saw.

In public they were oblivious to the stares or comments from people who saw them, but they still sought out those places where they could be alone. In movie theaters, the small girl would sit on her lap when the lights dimmed and whisper to her about what was happening on the screen. She liked the weight of the small girl on her legs and torso, and the ease with which the small girl balanced herself so she could watch the movie. She knew contentment at times like these with the small girl, and her days passed by pleasantly and without incident. Even so, the enervating awareness of blindness, the veil of her childhood, could make itself known even if she was doing exactly what she wanted. She did not talk about this with the small girl, though she wondered if the small girl sensed its presence; sometimes when the veil was most with her the small girl would make a valiant effort to tell an exciting story or suggest an adventurous walk to go on.

He also sometimes went to the movies – in the darkness and anonymity they offered he would wait for the lights to go down to take his seat, and once his eyes had adjusted glance at the people near him. They had their focus elsewhere and might not notice, which allowed him a rare opportunity to study people unimpeded. He could not look too long, however, and if people looked back at him he had to move.

On one night he sat down and when he could see in the mostly deserted theater he looked to his left – she was two seats over with the small girl on her lap whispering in her ear. There was enough light for him to tell that the small girl was looking at him, but not enough to see her expression, and if it was the usual reaction of violation and disgust. "What is it?" she asked, since the small girl had stopped whispering. The small girl said, "The man that is sitting by us -- he doesn't want to be seen." "What a shame," she said whispering back to the small girl, and without any thought reached her arm around the small girl's bony flank. He looked at her arm – long and pale in the low light, well-shaped – and then at her face, which was illuminated in profile by a brighter scene in the movie. She was wearing dark glasses. She turned her head slightly in his direction, then tilted her head upward, then left, paying no attention to the images on the screen. The little girl on her lap had stopped looking at him and was watching the movie and talking to her in a hushed voice. She must be blind, he thought.

He never stayed until a movie was over and the lights came up, but he waited this time to see what they would do. When the movie ended he asked her how she liked it. She smiled and angled her head his way but said nothing – she usually didn't talk to strangers and waited for the small girl to speak. He asked if they went to the movies often. She turned to the small girl, who had shifted her body so she could face him; the small girl stared at him, expressionless, and was silent. He asked if he could go with them to the movies some time. She again waited for guidance from the small girl but there was none. He talked to her as the theater emptied and said he could arrange to meet them in a few days – she could not recall anyone talking to her with such anticipation and urgency. She told the small girl it was what she wanted, and they left the theater together, the small girl taking her hand instead of climbing on her shoulders. She told him they lived with others in a house, and so he would know the location for the next time they met he walked back with them.

With only the small girl's hand to guide her, she moved hesitantly, and at one point absently reached out her other hand. He took it. They walked in this fashion back to her house, slowly, with the small girl giving little cues for directions to her but not speaking or looking at him. She noticed the heat and strength of his grip compared to the cold night air. He watched where they were headed but often looked at her features as the nighttime lighting periodically brought her into view.

After they had said their goodbyes and he had reluctantly given back her hand, he exulted over their meeting, throwing his fists into the air. She does not know the leer! She cannot see it, hear it or feel it! Over his whole life, he had not thought of a blind woman for himself, and he did not know why, but it didn't matter now. He imagined her finding pleasure in his touch, his voice, his desires as no woman ever had. The thought of her touch as she simply grasped his hand was an aphrodisiac that night and the following night as he waited to see her again, and planned for how he could have other subsequent meetings, have her back at his place, win her trust, make love to her, get her to fall in love with him. He worked on the timing and logistics of going out with her, how he could arrange his work life to spend time with her, how his place could accommodate her. Hours spent in his pretend world were replaced by details, strategies and his arousal fueled by hope long destroyed and deserted. His grim day-to-day existence, even his status as an outcast, felt like it might possibly, miraculously, be over.

It was not long before they were together all of the hours he could spare. As time passed the small girl removed herself more and more and did not accompany them when they were out. She missed the small girl but knew he was drawn solely to her, so she tried to understand how the small girl felt and why she might not want to be with her anymore. She became dependent on the small girl less and on him more. The first time they were alone in his apartment they made love for many hours, and he arranged for her to move in with him. She was unsure but when her parents objected she had the resolve to do it to defy them and further emancipate herself. Their caution and coldness was the antithesis of his passion and brazenness, and it was what drew her to him.

She relished the abandonment of convention and restriction during their sex, the shouting and pushing, moaning and giggling, prodding and screaming – they were not curious echoes from an air shaft but noises and feelings more akin to the playground scraps and dog piles that had attracted her at the school. He wanted to get as close as he could to her even as he was inside of her, his face pressed to her neck, her breast, her ear, her mouth, his breaths warming her skin and filling her lungs at the expense of his own. Her rapture was in plain sight and yet he pushed for more closeness, more evidence, that she was party to his desire and unaware of his accursed look. She leaped and grabbed at his efforts, the squeezing out of the space between him and her, the movement reducing the darkness she felt and even occasionally puncturing the implacable veil with daggers of what seemed like light. He did not trust that she was unperceiving of the leer and went to every length in their love-making to prove otherwise. She did not care about motives or virtue or anything else that was secondary to their coming together and frictioning off the black, spirit-obliterating veil that seemed more tenuous now than it ever had been.

The hours they were separated were glutted with smells and memories of their sex, and they fell into each other the moment he came back to the apartment. They each had one thing the other could not do: He would not let her run her hands over his face; and she would not open her eyes to him. He was concerned her hands were well attuned to reading the landscape of faces, and was afraid what her hands could find out about his features. She assumed her useless eyes were ugly and was afraid if she opened them he would no longer desire her. In all other areas, they found no limits to their sexual explorations. When they were physically spent, they kept close but said little. He would not talk about his life because it was about living with the leer which she did not know about and he did not want her to know about. She wanted to savor the experiences they had and didn't mind the silence.

When they went out it was at night, to the movies, or to parks where no other voices could be heard, often in bad weather when others were not out. Essentially, on these occasions they were still alone and apart from other people. Many days passed when the rest of the world did not matter to either of them. In time, though, she asked if he had friends, and he told her he had none. When she asked about going to new places, he said he did not want to do that. She told him she missed the small girl, but he reminded her that she had willingly withdrawn, had chosen to leave her alone – he hoped this would suffice, remembering how the small girl had stared at him when they met at the movie theater. What he did not tell her was that he feared if she knew how others reacted to him, she would loathe him as every other woman did. She did not know his motives, but she recognized as their isolation continued that he didn't want her around other people.

When he left for work she eventually tried to leave the apartment on her own – she had learned the layout and made her way to the front door. It was locked and she could not figure out how to open it. Feeling vexed she ran her hands across the floor and over the tabletop and countertop surfaces searching without success for a phone. She went to the windows, which were closed and would not open. She worked her way around the exterior walls of the apartment in hopes of coming across a back door, but did not. Sitting exhausted and frustrated on the floor, she felt her chin descending to her chest in a familiar pose of defeat.

After many minutes some far-off activity sent a vibration through the apartment that she picked up in her body where she sat. She remembered the reverberations of the husky-voiced older girl slapping the floor to find her way as well as the rapid footfalls of the small girl running toward her. They energized her and brought to bear her ingenuity and insubordination. She got up and found some of his tools in the bottom of his clothes closet – when he came back she had pried the front door open with a crow bar and was sitting on the doormat just outside. Her expression was one he had not seen before, a mixture of anger and obstinacy. He panicked and spoke quickly and incautiously, out in the hall within earshot of neighbors. He told her the locks were for her protection. He told her the neighborhood was not safe and he worried about her. He said he would make enough money to never have to leave again. He said if what she wanted was to travel the world, they would do that and she could invite as many friends if she wanted. He told her anything he could think of to keep her. And then she was willing to come back in and calmed down they made love and he tried to fulfill her so completely that she would not want anything else.

While he had been panic-stricken finding her outside the door, in fact whenever he was gone he worried about people coming to the door, her parents tracking her down, her losing interest in him because he was not there. Sometimes walking down the street he would think he saw the small girl in his peripheral vision, but when he turned to look there was no one. He went by the halfway house and watched to see if the small girl was around, but soon realized he was wasting time when he should be home.

Sometimes he would wake up in the middle of the night, turn on the light, pull back the covers on the bed and look at her. Some of those times he would be compelled to rouse her and make love to her. He was comfortable with her closed eyes and was glad of it, wondering at times what would happen if she stared straight at him in bright light – would some part of his prurient look filter through, would it awaken her dead senses, would she flee at this first sight of him. He kept the windows draped and lights off most of the time, and liked most being with her in complete darkness.

When it was night a desire came up in him to confess his real condition, how he was despised and shunned, how he rued the day when she would also recognize his leer and be repulsed. It felt like a life-threatening urge, standing on a ledge wanting to jump and lose

80

everything, to say these things to her. But his hand would stretch out to her in bed, caressing any part of her he wished, and it banished the thought of speaking up and losing moments like these. She, too, delighted in the caresses but it was the earlier moment, when he would grow still, take a sharp breath to talk but instead hold his tongue and touch her, that caught her attention. She was afraid to ask him about it. And then they would fall into each other and that was what mattered. When he made promises he did not keep, though, or lied about the locks or the phone, she wanted him to be plain with her. I want you for myself. I won't let you away from me. Painful words, but what she most wanted to hear, like the teacher's words "You are blind" that her parents could not say. She knew she could find a way to be free, it was a craving in her that was boundless, but she desperately wanted to know something else: If she had to give up her freedom for the furious, fiery closeness with him that might, in some mysterious, wondrous way, drive away the veil forever.

As time went on, she felt as if she could scarcely move at all. They were so close all the time she had almost had no space to herself. The apartment was the sum of their existence and it seemed she would never hear of another place or another person. She felt the veiled blackness around her as thin and vulnerable as she had ever experienced it, yet she also longed for the small girl and the open-ended wanderings they had shared and even the sad times when she was by herself in an empty room bemoaning her fate. For his part, he sensed her ignorance of him and his true nature was coming to an end, and he no longer cared about subterfuge or promises to forestall the inevitable – he simply wanted to be with her every moment until the moment that she would be gone. He felt powerless even as he exerted his will over her. And she despaired over the possibility that the world was not worth seeing if the price paid was too great.

One day, in bed, embracing each other, she put her hands on his face – he no longer stopped her, wanting every second of her time even if it took her a step closer to knowing his secret and leaving him. She poured over every curve and crease on his face in a way that might have aroused him before but now was mere sensation. Finally she brought her hands to rest, and said to him, "It's gone." For an instant he had no idea what she was referring to, but before he could ask he felt the blood rush into his cheeks where her hands lay, and he wondered about something so impossible and yet so ardently wished for he could not speak. He bolted from the bed, beside himself, unable to immediately find a light switch in the room amid the darkness. But he tripped over a flashlight and carried it to the mirror on the wall where he shined it up into his face, creating an oval of bright light and shadows, and then shined it directly into the mirror until it reflected onto his face with softer light. He rarely looked at his face, the source of his misery, and now felt ill-equipped to know something that should be obvious – that by some miracle his leer was gone. Behind him he could hear her sobbing on the bed and when he was exasperated at looking at himself he went back and placed her hands on his face again and asked her what she had meant. "It's gone," she repeated, softly and sadly, patting his cheeks and chin and forehead, taking breaths to push back the tears. She said the small girl had told her the night they had met that he had more desire than any other person she had seen, and that it was written in the lines and textures of his face. But there was no sign of it now, she said, mournfully.

She wondered if there was anything else to do. Holding her breath she positioned herself face to face with him and opened her eyes. Nothing. No bright shards piercing the veil now, no filmy vestiges – darkness was its primal impenetrable self. "The desire is gone," she said, voice trailing. She slumped back on the bed.

He shook his head, struggling with what was possible in the world. Slowly he took in her meaning – she had been aware all of their time together, of what he thought he had to hide above all else. She had not been oblivious to what marked him and tormented him, but had been drawn to it, had loved it, wanted more of it, and now mourned it. If the leer was gone, he had what he had wanted for as long as he had lived; and yet, her voice carried a sadness he couldn't endure. He realized he still had a flashlight in his hand and threw it as hard as could against a wall, extinguishing it.

She could think of nothing else except to move. She rose and reached for her clothes around the bed. The sound of her fingers tediously buttoning a shirt and tying shoes was excruciating to him. As he heard her feet touch the floor he called to her and slid over to the edge of the bed to feel her, and when he could not he reached out in vain and then lunged in her direction in the darkness. He tried to wrap his arms around her but instead knocked her over. She wanted to move and be free and crawled on all fours away from him, but he grabbed her ankles, and spoke to her again, begging her to come back to him. He slid his hands up from her ankles to her upper legs, then grabbed her waist and pressed his body forward against hers until he found her wrists and held them in his hands, pulling her back in the direction of the bed. She had not been held by her wrists like this since childhood, and the twisting and burning on her skin, the memory of being restrained and held against her will, triggered an awful brightness in her head. Suddenly she was once again the mad, implacable little girl, enraged at being trapped, singled out, and afflicted. She summoned her frustration and fury to break his grasp. She exploded with anger and screamed at him, pummeling his face with her hands.

Her response stunned him – so many women had threatened to punch him, kick him, punish him, but it had never happened, and as it now did, he did not defend himself. In fact he found that he believed he was owed these blows, that they were long past due. He did nothing to stop her. Her punches seemed to quiet his mind for the first time in a long while, and he briefly fantasized he had impelled her to hit him, invoking his long-dormant alter ego Sweet who could make anyone do his bidding. Unlike Sweet, however, he felt loathsome and pathetic. Even a woman who could not see him could not stand him.

As she flew at him she noticed a bright blur, dancing and jumping like she sometimes experienced in dreams. Her head tilted side to side and the blurry light followed her motions, rising and lowering in intensity with her wild swings and ragged screams. At some point she discovered her eyes had opened and she sensed something in the center of a blur: a frail shape, dimly lit, calm. It must be him, she thought. She did not dare blink for fear of losing the blurry image with him in the center. Her anger drained away and she put down her arms and breathed and peered in his direction.

He had lost track of thoughts and then consciousness, and did not open his eyes for a long time. When he finally opened his eyes he could not see. He was on his back near the bed, and she was talking to him sweetly, and then later she was helping him to his feet. He felt like a child, led around the apartment and then out onto the street. By then with the added light he thought he could see shapes and outlines, but not details. People's faces were vague rings of activity, nothing more. The faces he had spent so many hours of his life scanning and gauging and dreading were indecipherable. He was surprised to find he was not upset about his vision. Maybe it was because he was now oblivious to the judgment of others and all that wondering and suffering was over.

Maybe it was because at long last he felt looked after and cared for, loved in the way he had wanted his whole life.

As a couple they walked through a mass of people, she leading him slowly and carefully. She was sure she would have been terrified of the maelstrom of new images if not for the shape of him she could find in the middle of everything. And he felt unburdened – his fears and offenses for all to see, and it did not matter. He exhaled loudly, satisfyingly. She'd never heard him sigh before and mistook its meaning. "You will get your sight back," she reassured him. "I did."

THE BEAR

A middle-aged man is told by his doctor that he has only a short time to live. After he hears the diagnosis – a blood disease for which there is no cure – he goes home to look at financial arrangements that need to be made. As an insurance man, who inherited his father's business, he is well situated for death and has the proper documents in place. He expects to be comforted by the paperwork but in fact it feels like ash in his hands. When he replaces them in a file cabinet he expects it to tip over and crash, because that is how he feels – a tall tree rotten through the middle, waiting for a gust of wind to break it off at the root line. And then he does pull the cabinet over, with some pleasurable effort, until it crashes against his desk and sends a lamp and his father's old dictionary stand sliding to the carpeted floor. Just the thought of doing that would have chastened him before, such was his timidity. But he likes the loud sound he'd made, and the wish he has to make more just like it, whatever the consequences. He sees at his feet a fountain pen, a favorite of his mother's; he picks it up and breaks it into pieces. His anger is not directed at the doctor or the disease he said would kill him, or even at his parents who he lived with and took care of for so long; but at Trust and Reassurance, twin gods of do-gooders who promised him rewards for right-living and self-sacrificing that should have included long life but evidently did not.

With those totems fading from view, other gods lay right behind them, with new advice: Do whatever the hell you want. For similar instructions he has to turn his mind back to when he was sixteen on a class trip and drunk for the first time, wandering city streets in early

86

morning and shouting at some street toughs. But then he imagined his parents lost of two sons, the younger one at birth and the older one in bravado, and he turned away, silently and grimly, to resume his dutifulness. Now, decades later, there they are, back from the grave, the reckless things he might do.

All those years of minding and helping he had not truly felt like a caring person – not during the lawn mowing or gutter cleaning or even the shopping errands and hospital visits – but was always taken for one. People mistook his activity for a virtue, his behavior as selfless devotion to his mother and father rather than a child's compliance that unfurled into years of rote living. His reputation in the neighborhood, where he had lived his whole life, was for old-fashioned manners and values that now felt like products of fear and cowardice. And after his parents died, nothing had changed. Independence and inheritance, payoffs for being a dutiful son, could not change the course of his life; too much water had passed, the river dug too deep. He lived in the same house, parked in the same driveway. His life and theirs were shot through with spirit-sucking alarm clocks, TV trays and to-do lists treated like religious artifacts. People like them were one-act tragedies that turned into comedies, with pious obituaries and modest headstones serving as punch lines.

But he was done with his part, he could tell by the ideas floating around in his head.

In the backyard of his home, the ancestral home, as it were, he builds a bonfire. Armfuls of old musty clothes, the clawfoot piano bench with sheet music hidden under the seat, scrupulously marked boxes of Christmas decorations, an avocado colored can opener, quilts, throw rugs and door mats, alphabetized cassettes, the plastic-wrapped love seat, framed proverbs on hearth and home, a collection of hand-painted porcelain cups and saucers, magazines and books seldom read or never meant to be read. Untouched, all of it, following his parents' deaths, but still full of a stultifying sameness that completed his picture of himself not as a righteous, stay-behind son but a shuffling, spellbound ghost, unable to set foot outside the family mausoleum. Pitching the last load onto the fire was liberating and intoxicating, the noxious black smoke rising out of a smoldering, spitting mass and diffusing into the air and the noses of his neighbors. Noisy and dirty his last chapter would be. The slate wiped clean by a half-burnt tea towel covered in soot.

Into the void came first a black leather jacket – he is thrilled how heavy and smelly it is when he picks it up at a second-hand store, a perfect reminder of how things are going to change. Then he spends his money on a motorcycle – it is hard to handle and makes his ears ring and shoulders hurt, but he loves it. Rather than go into the office he waits to catch the teenage kid down the block who never seems to be doing anything, and asks him if he has any pot. Of course he does, and he sells a big bag of it to him, and when he spies the water pipe the kid has partially hidden in his bedroom closet, he buys that, too. He had never smoked pot, and had to ask how to work the pipe, but it doesn't take long until his heart is pounding, the blank silhouettes on the walls where his parents' framed proverbs were are fascinating and the story of his sad life is an absurd and twisted fairy tale.

When he comes down just a bit he rides to the darkest, saddest looking bar he can find and buys everyone in the place a drink. There are only two women that appear single, and after several drinks he propositions the older, tougher, less attractive of the two, thinking she might be more likely to accept, and he is right – she knows how to get on the back of his motorcycle and hang on, and he screams back into his neighborhood at closing time and shows her his emptied-out house. They smoke a bowl together in his bedroom and she passes out. He lifts her into his bed and when she wakes up they make love. He had rarely, and clumsily, had sex before and never in his home and never like this. He is harder than he has ever been and comes twice before they are through. Then he falls asleep and awakens to find her gone along with the money he'd had in his pockets. Money well spent, he thinks, happy to see his motorcycle still out front and his leather jacket on the floor of the hallway. He somehow remembers to call in sick to work and goes out for breakfast, where on route he is pulled over by a cop for speeding and riding without a helmet. The restaurant he picks has little candles on the tables, no bigger than votives, and he asks if his could be lit, whereupon he burns up the ticket.

Later that night he rides to the part of town where he had seen women staring into cars looking like prostitutes. He stops by the one who catches his eye and acts most inviting. After he solicits her, she asks him to wait in a nearby alley and when she returns she has a thick-necked cop with her and they put him under arrest. He pushes the beefy cop to see what will happen but the cop merely glares at him. They take him to the police station and he spends the night there. Because he has no prior record, he is released the next day, pending arraignment. He has no interest in spending his last days in court or in jail, and plans to leave. Someone from his work shows up at his house, and he sends him away. "Adios," he says, and then it occurs to him he should go to Mexico. He puts what he wants in a backpack and heads south. He has never been to Mexico and hated his Spanish teacher in school but assumes his money will go far down there and the police and his office staff will not pursue him. After two days of riding his body aches so he goes to an emergency room and convinces them he is dying so they prescribe him some painkillers. Now the miles evaporate on the road and he sleeps well in the motels along the way. One clerk admires his wristwatch and he gives it to him. Life is much easier this way, he thinks.

At the border he expects to be questioned but they wave him through. He stops a few hundred yards into Mexico to look back at the crossing, the stalled line of drivers pointed north, the glum-faced officers facing them, and beyond that the country he's happily left behind. A group of Mexican boys gather around him who speak English, and one of them looks at him and says, "Easy getting in, hard getting out." He finds this hysterical and gives each boy some dollars, and asks where he can buy peyote – the woman he'd brought home had said peyote was more fun than pot. They all speak at once and have suggestions but the boy who made him laugh looks at him seriously and writes a word down on his palm – curandera – telling him how to find this healer woman who can help him. To his amazement he is teary and wants to hug the boy but he runs off to another American who has stopped. He gives him his gloves instead and before the others can descend on him again he roars away.

He is sure he will get lost yet after following the boy's directions as best he could there is the street with the spiny plant fence – the boy had called it ocotillo -- and the house with the yard full of little figures. A long line of people outside are waiting, some with obvious afflictions – racking coughs, wayward eyes, weeping wounds, swollen limbs that have to be supported. A woman holding a rosary turns to him as he approaches and says, "Curandera," smiling and nodding. He goes to the door and asks if he can just ask a question and then he will be on his way. He is brought into a hall where money is taken and subsequently ushered into a living room with two women. Oddly, it reminds him a little of his parent's living room except for the window sill covered with colorful objects and a well-worn couch with a pile of pomegranates on it.

The older woman is of indeterminate age, with red-dyed hair, a weathered, round face, and very rough hands when she reaches out to greet him. She is wearing a green stone pendant over a cream-colored sweatshirt and sweatpants. Looking at him she speaks Spanish and the young woman by her says to him in English, "What do you want?" The older woman looks at him while the younger woman is distracted and pays him little notice – she is pretty, dressed in jeans and a T-shirt and acts bored. Casting his eyes back and forth between the two women he asks the older woman if he can buy peyote from her. The young woman is suddenly disgusted, saying they are not drug dealers, you stupid American, tells him to leave and pushes past him heading toward the hall. But the older woman is still staring at him and has noticed he looks unperturbed by her assistant's reaction. She says "¿Por qué has venido?" dropping her head a bit and after a pause adds "Why come?" He shrugs his shoulders and says, "Why not?" then exclaims, "Yes, why not!" He is surprised he remembers some Spanish from school. The curandera motions the younger woman to return. She says quite a bit, which the young woman, still miffed, indifferently translates, but he does hear that he should go find a man that the healer knows. He is a wild man who has what he seeks – the man lives outside of civilization. He starts to ask about the peyote and she says through the young woman that the man knows where to find such things, and knows many other ways to get away. He looks confused at the translation and young woman, with scarce patience, says, "You lose yourself, Druggie. Abandono." The curandera pulls a small notepad out of her pocket and spends a full minute writing something on a little sheet of paper that she gives to him. He looks at it – the writing looks like neither English nor Spanish. This is to give to the man when you find him, the young woman translates. Before he can ask, she says

91

he lives in the desert, and tells him the name of the closest town. "How will I find him," he asks? The curandera looks at him and shrugs her shoulders. "Maybe you won't," the young woman says.

With a great deal of difficulty the man finds the town on the edge of the desert. He uses almost the last of his dollars to buy provisions and drive his motorcycle on the one road leading into the desert. It is marked by potholes and tire tracks that gradually fade as the road narrows. He likes the column of dust the motorcycle leaves swirling in its wake. The earth is by turns dusky red and chalk white but turns gray once in the air. After some miles the engine dies and can't be restarted. He drinks water and tequila by the side of the road and wonders about walking back into town and forgetting about the peyote. Come on a whim and leave on a whim, he thinks to himself; that's the way I do things now. The tequila has mellowed him and he looks around. Except for scrubby brush by the road and mountains in the distance, there is nothing to see. It's dead quiet but for the rushing noise in his ears from the motorcycle. He had never been camping and never been in the desert. He starts walking back, dreaming of a soft bed, women and more tequila. It is hot, and his pack feels heavy. Now he is pissed off at the healer woman and her wild man who cannot be found and probably doesn't exist. I just want to get high, he says aloud. He turns around to see how much distance he has put between him and his motorcycle, and sees a dog trailing him. He looks again and guesses it is a coyote. Maybe this is how it ends, he says, throwing his tequila bottle toward the coyote, who just watches it crash into the ground nearby. He puts his head down and walks faster.

Soon it is dark and he keeps moving, expecting the town to appear ahead of him. At some point he notices he is off the road, walking on a path, and he doesn't know how long ago that happened

– he doubles back and then he isn't sure which direction the path leads. The temperature is dropping, he is lost, and for the first time in a long time he isn't sure what to do. He drops to his knees and pulls the leather jacket around him. He vaguely recalls hearing people surviving by walking all night but he is tired and drunk and wants to sleep off this major annoyance and get back in the morning. The plants near his feet smell like tar and his neck is on fire from sunburn. In a few hours he drifts into sleep but awakens shivering and coughing. He checks his watch for the time then remembers he gave it to the motel clerk. He is amused, if he doesn't survive the night, that the clerk has the watch.

There is no moon but hundreds of stars he cranes his neck to see. He feels very cold but doesn't particularly care. He drifts off again and in time is dimly aware of being lifted off the ground. It is like he is a child again being carried by his father to his room at bedtime. Strangely he doesn't mind. Something has him by the legs with his torso thrown over a bony shoulder. It's a fast, quiet step and he bounces with every footfall but feels almost nothing. What he is aware of, and barely so, beyond the muffled noise and numb pounding, is body odor stronger and different from his own. After some time he is suddenly dumped onto the ground – it's dark, still freezing cold, but not in the open air. His face is wet and he realizes it has smashed against a rock. The rank smell and soft noises, now at a distance, remain. Then a fire is lit and sharp sounds of crackling wood follow. It hurts to raise his head but he opens his eyes to see he is in a very dark space with shadows played on the walls. Crossing his field of vision is a man – too dark to make out any features. He can't keep his eyes open, can't focus or think about anything. Something heavy is tossed on him, covering him. As he warms up he falls asleep.

He wakes sweating, head throbbing, face itching from a thick blanket of fur on top of him. He is shrouded by an animal hide so heavy he wants to move it away from his face so he can breathe. Bristles stick to the caked blood on his cheek. When he opens his eyes he realizes the man he saw earlier is squatting over him. Now that there is more light he can see him – very lean, ropey muscles in his neck, hair and beard both matted and stringy, ocher skin, whites of his eyes so shot with blood that his pupils look pale by comparison. Naked except for an old shirt tied at his waist and a string of animal teeth around his neck. The wild man reaches down and feels the cut and dried blood he has on his forehead from the fall. The finger is as rough as an emery board and he recalls a trip to a carnival as a child, listening to a sideshow barker coax people to enter a tent to see someone called the alligator boy – "You could light a match on any part of his body, including his face." The wild man points to his own forehead, where he has a scar, a curved snake-shaped line even darker than his skin. It is hard to emerge from the animal hides, he is tired and hung over, and after falling back asleep he opens his eyes again to see the wild man looking at the curandera's note he had stuffed it into his pocket. After he is through he puts it into his mouth and swallows it.

He can't believe he has found the wild man, or rather, that the wild man has found, in fact rescued, him. It is more remarkable than locating the curandera; it seems beyond good fortune, that he was meant, after so many pedestrian years, to have some number of extraordinary experiences before he dies. He thought he might be sent to see a hermit, or an outcast of society, not somebody who seemed out of time, from another age. He is amazed, and wonders if it's possible he could be dreaming, or even if he has died already and entered some supernatural realm. But his aches and pains say otherwise. The wild man reaches down and with little effort pulls him to his feet, out of the animal skins. He has a terrifying thought – He will kill me – which is counter-weighted by another – I was sent here – that allows him to be calm enough to stay still when the wild man turns away. He is wary, but also interested. Insolence, his companion since building the bonfire, is gone, replaced by a not-unpleasant vigilance for what may next befall him.

The wild man does many things, some out of eyesight and thus more worrisome, but when he returns he comes with water to drink and meat cooked by the fire. That is reassuring, but soon thereafter the wild man leaves the cave not looking back, gone for the rest of that day and most of the night. He finds no other food, is hungry and cold and grows scared wondering when the wild man will return or even if he wants him to return. Be careful what you wish for, as his mother would have said. But he does return, stokes the fire, shares food, and touches his wounded forehead again perhaps as a sign of concern.

When the next dawn comes he is ready and follows him out of the cave. He has no idea if the wild man will object, or be indifferent and lose him somewhere along the way. None of those things occur. Before one day is through, he is petrified, fascinated, exhilarated, and many more emotions he cannot keep track of. The day feels like it lasts forever. And how many followed? He cannot keep track of that, either.

No words are ever exchanged – the wild man uses a language that is neither English or Spanish, and gets his intentions across by gestures and eye contact. When it is first light and still cold he puts the fire out and kneels silently by the smoke and ash. He hunts and scavenges over an expanse of many miles, sometimes resting in a thicket by water that attracts rabbit and quail. All things catch his attention, especially birds and trees, and when he finds particular plants, like dandelions, he exults, and when he passes through one canyon that looks like marble, he cries. On certain days he wipes both their faces with grease, and on moon-filled nights they forage making noises as they go. There is a low place with bubbling mud where bones of animals they have eaten are thrown, and there is a hillside where cactus of every shape, texture and flavor grow. The bitter, bulbous cactus they eat turns minutes into days and campfire flames into stories of a vanished world. He knows this is the drug he was seeking but in truth every experience in the desert is an intoxicant. He follows the wild man like a child not wanting to be left behind, climbing, crawling, creeping or racing, cutting his feet and hands but excited by what he is capable of. He watches what the wild man does, awkwardly but eagerly trying his knots, grips, throws, and thrusts. He aches with hunger and thirst long enough to savor brackish water and sour berries. He suffers sunburns by how welcome they will be in the freezing night air. He sleeps in perpetual dreams and sexual arousal with the smoke and cold and smell of his own body buried in the animal skins wrapped around him.

One day in brush by a ravine he sees the wild man diverted by a scratching sound, which causes him to unsheathe a knife and slowly step in the direction of the noise. The wild man waves a hand in his direction then holds it still. He steps quietly through the thicket until he runs into the open, to where a javelina is digging into the ground with its snout. The wild man tackles and repeatedly stabs the animal, which struggles and squeals and gores him until it is finally subdued. The wild man ignores his wound and quickly cuts up the pig – they eat some in the clearing and carry the heavy carcass back to the cave, where they cook and eat much of the rest. He almost expects his stomach to burst from all the unexpected meat, but when the wild man jumps up and down and shouts with pleasure he joins him. They make sounds to each other until he can't come up with another note or another noise to imitate; they shake and stamp feet, grasp arms to dance in circles, take turns leaping over the fire and hurl embers against the cave walls spraying themselves with spark and ash. His old way of living enters his mind to say, we should reserve food, save energy for tomorrow, but it is fleeting. He can't recall when he was less self-conscious and more exuberant. Gradually, they both wind down with the fire and fall asleep.

He rouses at dawn deeply contented. But he is also aware in those moments of his mortality. Not just the knowledge of the doctor and the fatal disease, but what he is gaining from the wild man in the desert, and how little time he may still have to gain more of it. Lying warm in the animal skins, he has a reverie, of learning everything about this new world, if he could only live long enough to do it. Because the curandera sent him here, she must have knowledge of mysteries, calamities, infirmities as well as their remedies. Perhaps she has a potion or treatment that would give him more time, or perhaps even cure him, he wonders, so he can learn all of the wild man's ways of the desert. From the doctor he had seen, he learned little or nothing, certainly not how long he might live; now he was glad how unhelpful the doctor and modern medicine had been, since he had found aid elsewhere, on his own. Somehow the curandera intuited he wanted nothing to do with his old life and craved new experiences, and she knew where he could find them; if she knew that, she could know other secrets, including how to make him healthy and free of disease. He would have loved to ask the wild man what he knew about the curandera, but that was impossible; he was left instead with just one idea of what he should do.

He had glimpsed the road he had come in on from a hill they had climbed. It was a distant, distasteful memory, and he was not happy to have spied it, as part of the natural landscape they inhabited. But now he quietly gathers things while the wild man sleeps and heads for the road, unfazed by the difficulties ahead and motivated by what the curandera might have to offer him.

After an untold number of arduous days and the aid of several Samaritans, who saw he had nothing and wished only to see the curandera, he returns to the street of the ocotillo fence and the house with the yard of little figures. There is a line of people waiting to be healed and this time he takes his place in line though he feels impatient as the time passes and he is so close to his destination. As they inch forward he notices some people are being paid to stand in line for someone else and look over their shoulder for their patrón; he could see people from every walk of life sought the curandera's help. He is anxious to see her himself and for a moment regrets the money and standing he has forsaken, for he would use them to make his wait shorter. It is just that I am tired, he tells himself.

After a long while he is ushered into the living room again and the curandera enters by herself. He is not sure whether she will understand him without a translator but he cannot wait further. He tells her how he desperately hopes she can treat or even eradicate his disease so he can live longer and learn to hunt animals, forage for roots and berries, start fires from stone and tinder and want for nothing from the outside world. He praises her wisdom and knowledge, her ability to heal people with medicines no doctor could know, and is still beseeching her when she raises her hand to stop him from continuing. She says, in a mix of English and Spanish he understands, "Go back to the wild man – your cure is there." She starts to walk out – in a panic that comes over him he grabs her arm and says "Por favor" several times and drops to his knees, clasping his hands in front of him, closing his eyes with deference but also fear that he will open them and she will be gone. But she is there when he looks up at her again – she looks younger and more attractive than he remembers, and he wishes he would have washed before he arrived and made a better impression, and could spend more time in her presence, because he had forgotten what it was like to be in the presence of a woman. She looks at him as well, intently, just as she had when he was first there, but will say no more, and walks out.

This time he does not try to detain her; he is so crushed by what has happened he needs to be helped to his feet by others and moved to an adjoining room, where he lies until asked to leave at sunset.

He lingers outside, distraught and confused. He thinks about sleeping by the house, waiting to see her the following day. But he does not believe she will help him further. He cannot conceive that the wild man has his cure, even if he could communicate this dire need to him, which he can't imagine being able to do. The hope that propelled him out of the desert and back to the curandera is gone. He is exhausted and hungry and despondent. Death, which had seemed far away, feels close by. There is an encampment near the house of others like himself and he goes there, collapsing by a fire, not sure if he will be able to get up. In the morning, though, given food and clothing by those who took pity on him, he rises, and looks off in the two opposite directions that he had come from that each time had led him to the curandera's house. He kicks at a stone by his feet, which spins in the dirt for a second or two and ends up pointing in the direction of the desert.

Not knowing what else to do, he begins to retrace his route back to where the wild man lives. There is no coyote on the road this time but instead a raven with its impassive gaze perched in a creosote bush. He does not know if he will make it back, and yet over the course of time he notices he is surrounded by the parts of the desert he recognizes. He passes places he has been and thinks about looking for the cave where they stayed when he sees the wild man. As their eyes meet the wild man shows only the slightest recognition, and seems uninterested when he follows him. He realizes how weak he has become as he has difficulty keeping up.

About the time he feels he can go no further and stops, at the moment he feels as vulnerable as he has ever been, the wild man doubles back and, instead of lending aid, turns on him, attacks him, grabs him by the throat. He is shocked and meekly defends himself, but soon with the wild man's strength upon him he cannot breathe and is convinced he will succumb at any moment. Suddenly he is fighting for his life, calling on energy he did not know was there, trying to break free, stay conscious. The face of the wild man is as it was the first day in the cave, strange and remote but with an admixture of caring, even as he now applied pressure and tightened his grip. He strains with every bit of himself to resist, one more moment, one more effort; abruptly, as if in response, the wild man smiles at him, releases his grip and embraces him instead, wrapping his strong arms around him. He shouts and laughs, patting his back, lifting him up off the ground, and he is too weak to resist and happy for it besides – he is alive. The wild man then leads him to a place where there is meat and fruit stored underground. Finding strength in defense of his life and being welcomed at last and fed by the wild man invigorates him.

Shortly thereafter they leave, heading toward higher ground. The wild man leads him to a small mountain cave, overlooking a valley, where there are makings of a fire just outside the entrance. They take honeycombs from a nearby tree and eat them by the flames of a newly made fire. The wild man fashions torches from the fire and they sit in the open air, where it is twilight. As daylight fades he gives him cactus to eat and takes some himself. Afterwards, using the torches to light the way, they find a trail that circles the mountain. He follows the wild man for what seems like hours in a dream state until they reach a spring-fed pool. The air is warm and heavy with an acrid mineral odor. He can't see well; the steam rising from the water surface reflects off the light from his torch. The wild man is ahead of him, already in the water, and he can just make out his outline.

Incredibly, he sees other movement in the pool, of someone else, partly submerged. The wild man appears to wade toward the other person, low in the water, and they become intertwined, vague shapes obscured but also animated by the steam. He must be hallucinating, he thinks, entering the water himself. It is hot and glides over his skin like oil. He forgets about his torch and it extinguishes it in the pool. Now that it is dark and he no longer can see, he can hear them, rhythmically panting and rippling the water. He steps cautiously on the slick rock beneath his feet, moving slowly toward the sound with trepidation and curiosity. When he is near he stops, closes his eyes, and listens. There are two voices, different in pitch, soft and ecstatic, sounding without words, inhuman and intimate, wild and erotic to him in proximity to it.

Quiet comes, and he opens his eyes – he can see a little now in the dark, and the wild man drops down into the water, off to the side, then disappears. He instinctively moves forward, toward the other, and this is reciprocated. Before he knows it he is engulfed in a feminine presence – soft, knowing hands, sweet, musky smell, the low murmur of desire, urgent without haste, everything he desired desiring him. As he is being touched he reaches out, to her face, her breasts, her waist, everywhere smooth and warm. She is familiar, the one he has always wanted, but exotic and ineffable as well, a stranger with a resemblance to a long-lost love. He grabs her long, full hair, her thin arms and wide hips, looking into eyes he cannot see that he knows are cast over him all the while. Reaching behind her, his hands gliding over her skin, moving yet closer, he feels his erection slide into her, naturally, astonishingly, beautifully. All his senses focus there, at the joining, though he is so close to her they touch in many places and her leavened breath he can feel on his cheeks and in his nostrils. He is in a place with no bearings, like before he was born, except not alone, she is there connected to him, wordlessly and effortlessly and sublimely present, when it started and when it completes, the rising and lowering, coupling and uncoupling, and with the end the coming back into his mind and senses. She retreats into the mist and, in time, he goes to the edge of the spring. The wild man is gone. He lies in a stupor, staying warm in the coldest hours, then at first light finds his own way back to the high cave. The experience with the woman sits on his skin like the slick mineral water and he has no wish to lose it -- he does everything he can to not think, not ask questions, not do anything but walk back where he can rest and delight in his experience.

Outside the cave he sees the wild man has made two fires next to each other. One smolders, half-smothered with clothes he wore when he first came into the desert – he had no idea the wild man had saved these after he had discarded them. The other fire has charred bones from an animal in a bed of red coals still spitting from fat and sinew. They both are ringed with stones but otherwise seem to him from different worlds. As he studies the fires he comes to believe the wild man has built them to communicate this very idea to him, and more – that there are two distinct worlds, and they live in the vibrant one. He momentarily considers rescuing his old shirt and socks from the smoldering fire, thinking there must be some use in them still, and even that urge tells him that that fire is not his world, where he did not act with urgency or ingenuity, only bland practicality.

He kneels by the active fire, peers into it, leans into the heat – the coals flicker with a message he seems close to understanding. As he stares, caught up in the fire, he feels a connection with the wild world so strongly that he has left everything he once was behind. Stay in this world, and out of the other, he thinks, and civilization with its doomsday doctors and fatal blood diseases can't touch you. He reaches in and collects one of the charred bones, burning his hand. He holds it to his chest, hoping to leave a scar, marking his discovery. He is weary to the core, and full of dreams: He wants to thank the wild man, he wants to light a fire the size of a mountain, he wants to find the source of all springs in the depths of the earth.

Later that day, the wild man returns but acts spent and so they lay low for some hours, which is unusual. The afternoon stretches out at its own pace. At sunset, a bear comes into the high cave where he and the wild man are resting. It canters in like it has been there before, or is attracted by strong smells or something else humans would not know, moving faster and quieter than such a huge creature could conceivably move. There is no time, nor the light, to see its features. The wild man leaps to his feet but the bear is already in the cave, and it is too late to react, or perhaps it is the wrong thing to react, as the bear responds by laying him open with one swipe of its enormous paw. The wild man, eviscerated, falls like a puppet off its string. Then, uneager and unhurried, the bear pushes its snout into the cavity it has created, and begins to eat.

He watches from where he is, further back in the cave, and the killing comes so swiftly and grotesquely he is paralyzed with terror; he feels himself grown cold and is not sure he is still breathing, and doesn't wish to, if it would attract the bear, but the bear ignores him. It finishes eating the wild man and casts what is left of him aside. Grunting and huffing, it clears a space in the cave. When it is through it drops down on its haunches and sniffs, but does not turn in his direction. Gradually the light recedes but the bear does not go. After countless excruciating minutes, afraid the bear will come for him in the dark, he hears the bear exert itself. The slightest glow of starlight had been visible at the cave's entrance but now is blacked out by the bear's great size. Rising on its massive legs, moving without haste, it lumbers into the open and is gone.

He cannot move his body until morning. Even though he was desperate to get out of the cave he still smelled the bear in the dark and saw it in his mind's eye, where it was not far away and there was no hope of escape. With light he is able to become unstuck mentally and physically, and crawls out into the sun. He is grateful for the warmth on his face, for the breaths he can take. His cheeks are wet, as if the sun were thawing out his frozen body, but he knows it is tears that are gratitude for surviving the night, and being part of this new day. His head wants to stay pitched back soaking in the sky but eventually comes down to earth to where he stands, outside the mouth of the cave. The fire rings are trampled, picked through. The wild man's gutted body is lying on nearby rock, with fresh wounds to the arms and legs. He wonders how coyotes or other animals could have scavenged in the night and he not heard them. Maybe it was the wind that came, that continues still, shielding him from other sounds.

A raven is partially obscured in sage plant by the rock – drawn to the corpse, no doubt, as would be the vultures as the day lengthened. He imagines the wild man would want his bones picked clean, but he will never know. He sobs, something he hasn't done since he was a little boy. Consoled by his mother then, now watched over by the raven, which is buffeted by the wind but unswayed in its attention to him in the throes of his crying. I probably sound like a bird, he thinks, staring at the raven, comforted. Bit by bit he picks through the remnants of the fires, retrieving his old shirt, singed but wearable, and the wild man's animal tooth necklace – it must have been mixed in with the bones he had seen in the fire. Both are warm, welcome. He looks out, as he has done before, beyond where he is, first the round-mountain trail, then the path down to the valley and the old cave, with the trace of a road leading out of the desert into the distance. "So much I don't know, except… I am dying," he says, out loud. The wind kicks up, cool against his face as a cloud covers the sun. "And the season is changing," he says, shifting his gaze to the raven, smiling in the midst of his teariness. "Find your nest when your business is finished." He turns to look back at the cave and laughs – a dark humor that does not bother him and reminds him of himself when he was picking up women and burning up speeding tickets. He is thankful it led him here, where his energy may be gone but the memory of it remains.

Slowly, with effort, he gathers the things that he wants and goes back into the cave. His activity flushed the raven out of the sage grass, or perhaps it was the raven's awareness of other animals – it would not surprise him if the bear was close at hand. He lies down where he had been and again feels fear, a familiar friend. He wants every second of this time, but it does not take long for the bear to return. Still it ignores him, reacquainting itself with space it had made for itself. The bear finds stones outside he did not know were there, and begins dragging them to the cave and closing the entrance. It grunts as it works like an old person and he finds that amusing but makes no noise, not wishing to break the spell of his invisibility. Finally, laboriously, it finishes its work, sealing off most of the light and creating a texture of air – more smell, more echo – that no longer feels like a cave, but is something new. The bear now seems tired, quieter, its mood softer. Perhaps he is imagining this, because it is how he feels. It sits at first, then collapses on its side, its prodigious bulk very close to him. He is so close the bear's slowing breath hits his cheek and its indescribable smell fills his nostrils. Then the bear pulls him in, effortlessly, into its infinite fur. One massive paw covers him, warming him. "I have finally been saved," he says.